50¢

Cameron's Troop Lift

Cameron's Troop Lift

Philip McCutchan

St. Martin's Press
New York

Library of Congress Cataloging-in-Publication Data

McCutchan, Philip, 1920–
    Cameron's troop lift.

    1. World War, 1939–1945—Fiction.   2. Great Britain—
History, Naval—20th century—Fiction.   I. Title.
PR6063.A167C36   1987   823'.914   87-13132
ISBN 0-312-01008-7

First published in Great Britain by George Weidenfeld & Nicolson Ltd.

First U.S. Edition

10 9 8 7 6 5 4 3 2 1

Cameron's Troop Lift

1

THE SKY above the destroyer was like lead: gone were the idyllic days – idyllic, that was, when the exigencies of war permitted – when the sun shone down from a brassy heaven as HMS *Caithness* lay alongside the berth in Trincomalee or carried out scouting missions into the Bay of Bengal, watchful for any forays by the Japanese from Java or Sumatra to the south-east and Burma to the north-east. The war's centre of gravity was shifting to the eastern seas as the Mediterranean passed back to Allied control and the Battle of the Atlantic turned against Hitler and Grand Admiral Raeder. Farther to the east, in the Pacific, the naval forces were building up, and a British Pacific Fleet was now added to the strong US presence in the area. Cameron had been one of those who had been withdrawn from the North Atlantic. He had proceeded by what was virtually a pierhead jump to take command of the *Caithness*, replacement for her previous captain killed in action against Japanese aircraft operating from an aircraft-carrier steaming unexpectedly west of Singapore. It was to be a different war from the one that Cameron had been fighting to date.

On his first arrival in Ceylon, the Deputy Chief of Staff at Naval HQ had remarked on this.

'You're used to convoys, Cameron, in the main.'

'Yes, sir.'

'You won't be employed on escorts out here. Independent

action's the order of the day. Patrols, probes against the Japs over there.' Captain Anderson had waved an arm towards the east, out across the Bay of Bengal and the Indian Ocean. 'You'll have heard stories about the Japs. They're a frantic lot . . . all that dedication, carried to extremes. Fanatics to a man.'

'I've heard of the *kamikaze* pilots,' Cameron said.

Anderson nodded. 'Yes. Human bombs that can't miss. Good thing our carriers have armoured flight decks! The Americans have suffered hell . . . wooden flight decks, and the buggers go through like a knife through butter. All that's in the Pacific, of course. With any luck, you'll have a quieter life operating out of Trinco – but don't quote me on that. We've had our casualties, as you know, of course.'

Cameron had left Naval HQ reflecting that once you'd been killed you might just as well not have been in a quiet area, and wherever you happened to be sent in this war you faced the prospect of sudden death from one form of attack or another. The civilian population back in Britain hadn't escaped: the London blitz, Coventry, Portsmouth, Southampton, Plymouth, the list was endless. It was dragging on and on and although light was at last dawning in the western hemisphere, daybreak in the east was still a very long way off. However, the words of the Deputy Chief of Staff had proved true so far: three patrols northward up the Bay of Bengal, three north-eastward towards the Andaman Islands, and never a sight of the enemy. It had been the time of the north-east monsoon, the fine, windless weather and the blue skies, and the enervating heat below decks where fresh air seemed seldom to penetrate and where in peacetime windscoops would be rigged in the scuttles, turned to catch any breeze made by the ship's way through the water.

But now the dry season was just about at an end. The south-west monsoon was upon them, bringing the dirty weather, the cold mugginess, the wind and the teeming rain. . . .

Cameron, on the forebridge as the watch changed at noon,

looked up at that leaden sky, down at the restless heave of the sea, changed from deepest blue to the same depressing colour as the sky. There was a curious feeling in the air, a kind of foreboding, an odd suspension of time and place as though the ship and her company were in limbo. Cameron remarked on this to the navigating officer, an RNR lieutenant named Dawnay.

'Too damn silent, Pilot. I'm used to the sound of the wind, when the sea and sky are like this.'

Dawnay nodded. 'It's not unusual here. I've known it enough times.' Dawnay, a professional seaman from the merchant service, had been in the British India ships before the war and the Indian Ocean was like his own back yard. 'When it comes at the change of the monsoons – '

'Like now.'

'Yes, sir. It can mean the wind'll be along shortly. When I say wind, I mean wind!'

'Hurricane?'

'Yes. Ever met one before, have you?'

'No.' Cameron gave a brief grin. 'But since I've been out here I've made a study of them.'

'In theory, sir.'

'Yes, but – '

'The practice can be different. Tropical cyclones . . . they can be unpredictable, don't always run true to theory.'

'Fill me in on them, Pilot.'

'Right, sir. In the Bay of Bengal they tend to move north-westerly from around the Andamans towards the mouth of the Ganges. The actual cyclone whirl is around sixty to eighty miles in diameter. The associated wind can reach a hundred miles an hour – '

'But the dead centre's calm, right?'

'Yes, that's right. And outside the violent blow, on the borders, the wind's light. So if we pick up a light wind – '

'That'll be the warning?'

'Yes, sir, it could be. But not necessarily. Every light wind doesn't have to mean a hurricane. On the other hand, I'd say that this time it does.'

'Because of the atmosphere, the quietness?'

'Yes. The calm before the storm, if you don't mind a cliché, sir.'

Cameron took up his binoculars and scanned the horizons all round. They were close and the overcast seemed to be increasing, and still there was no wind. No enemy either. Cameron said, 'Well, I'll not clamp everything down just yet. It's pretty hellish below as it is. You think we'll get fair warning, Pilot?'

Dawnay said, 'Yes, I think so. I'll be watching it, sir, don't worry.' He added, 'I believe there is a hurricane around somewhere, but it may not come our way. That's largely where the unpredictability comes in.'

Cameron turned for'ard, sat himself on the high stool in the fore part of the bridge and folded his arms on top of the screen. He sank his head broodingly on to them: the closeness of the atmosphere sapped men's strength and despite a surface coldness there was continual heavy sweating. It would be no better, probably worse, back in Trinco. No movement on the ship would mean no movement of air, not unless the hurricane, if it came, struck Ceylon, and then the only thing for the ships in the anchorage to do would be to go to sea and fight it out. No seaman liked the constriction of the land when a real storm hit. Cameron's father, himself a master mariner, had once been in Hong Kong when a typhoon blew up. He had taken his ship to sea . . . he had happened to have 'flu at the time but had refused to leave the bridge. His ship had taken a battering but had remained afloat, and after he had brought her in safely he'd gone down with double pneumonia and pleurisy. The Royal Naval hospital had pulled him through. So much for typhoons, which were the same as hurricanes, the name depending on which part of the world you were in. But his father's experience – he'd been very seriously ill – had remained in the juvenile Cameron's mind and had given him a possibly irrational-sized dislike of ever having to bring a ship through a hurricane himself. Or having to try: over the years many ships had in fact succumbed to hurricanes and typhoons, lost with all hands when the storm centre took them in its grip. Violent storms at sea could be more lethal than Hitler, more lethal than the Japs.

Waiting now for the first hint, the first puff of wind, Cameron, painfully aware of that lack of personal experience of hurricanes, knew one thing for certain and above all: none of his self-doubts must become visible to the ship's company. He, the Captain, was the one they all depended on; the decisions would be his alone. But he would be glad enough to have Dawnay's advice. As a lieutenant-commander RNVR Cameron was lucky to have command of even a small destroyer of the size of the *Caithness*: corvettes and trawlers apart, very few commands had gone to the RNVR; and Cameron was well aware that Dawnay could leave him standing when it came to sheer sea experience

ii

The threat of a hurricane had not been lost on the lower deck. Petty Officer Bustacle, chief bosun's mate – or buffer in the vernacular of the lower deck – had taken it upon himself to have a word with Lieutenant Main.

'First Lootenant, sir?'

'Yes, Bustacle.'

'Don't like the look o' the sky, sir. Due for a blow, sir, I reckon.'

'It just looks overcast to me.'

'Yes, sir. But there's more behind it. Bay o' bloody Bengal . . . funny part o' the world, sir.' Bustacle paused; he was well on the wrong side of forty, a time-expired reservist called back from pension just before the mobilization of the fleet and the outbreak of war back in '39, and like Dawnay he had plenty of experience, which in his view was more than could be said for Lieutenant Main. . . . Main was RN, ex Dartmouth, all very pusser and proud of a newly-acquired second stripe: six weeks ago he had been Sub-Lieutenant Main and his promotion, because he was a straight striper, made him automatically senior to any of the RNR and RNVR lieutenants, and in Bustacle's view that was a load of codswallop because Main scarcely knew the difference between a fairlead and a fuck. He needed prodding into everything. Now, Petty Officer Bustacle did some prodding. He said, 'Hurricanes, sir. If one comes, we just have to be ready like.'

'There's been no order from the forebridge, Bustacle.'

'No, sir, there hasn't, not that I know of. But the skipper, he'll expect us to be ready just the same.' Bustacle felt like adding, he'll expect it of *me* to be ready . . . but that could have sounded tactless when speaking to Jimmy the One.

'I see.' Main adjusted the set of his uniform cap, bringing the peak well down over his nose, which gave him a supercilious look since he had to put his head back to continue the conversation. 'What d'you suggest, Bustacle?'

'Usual bad-weather routine, sir, only a bit more so like. Deck gear ready. Extra strops for the anchors, overhaul the slips on the fo'c'sle, likewise the boats' falls, gripe-in the seaboat, tighten funnel stays – '

'I can't pass the gripes on the seaboat without orders from the bridge, Bustacle.'

'No, sir.' Bustacle gave a half-audible sigh: everyone knew that the point of the seaboat was that it was always kept ready for instant swinging-out and lowering, but at the same time the skipper wouldn't want to lose it and anyway you couldn't lower a boat in a hurricane. 'Be ready like, that's all, sir.'

Lieutenant Main frowned and pulled at his chin indecisively, then said, 'Yes, well. It might be a good idea, but leave the seaboat. See to it, will you, Bustacle?'

'Aye, aye, sir.' Bustacle turned about and went for'ard before Jimmy could change his mind, lose his nerve or whatever. Bustacle felt it in his bones that they were in for a nasty blow. He'd done his time China-side back in the middle thirties, and in Singapore as well, in a County Class cruiser, one of the old three-funnel jobs with high freeboard and a terrible propensity to roll her guts out at the drop of a hat.

10

She'd steamed smack into a typhoon on no less than three occasions in the South China Sea and although she had come through she'd sustained terrible damage on the upper deck, losing all her boats and once a funnel, even the gun-barrels in one of the 6-inch turrets twisted into knots, and there had been casualties to the ship's company as well, including Bustacle himself who'd broken a leg on the third occasion. Bustacle reckoned he knew something about typhoons and hurricanes, and one of the things he knew was when they were coming.

On his way for'ard he collected the fo'c'sle divisional PO, Tucker, like himself an RFR man. Together they climbed the starboard ladder to the break of the fo'c'sle and Bustacle repeated what he'd said to the First Lieutenant.

Tucker said, 'You really reckon a hurricane, Archie?'

'Yes.'

'There's sod-all wind. . . .'

'You wait, that's all.'

'What's Jimmy doing about it, then?'

Bustacle sucked at a hollow tooth. 'Gone below for the Brylcreem, case the bloody wind ruffles his hair. That apart . . . he's agreed we might as well be ready. Check all the fo'c'sle gear, will you, Ron? For my money, the order'll come from the bridge before we're much older.'

'Right you are, Archie.'

'Leave you to it, then.' Bustacle went back down the ladder after a quick look round the anchors and cables and the centre-line capstan, brake on and out of gear with the inboard ends of the cables wrapped around the cable-holders on their way down to the Senhouse slips in the lockers. As he moved aft towards the depth-charges the destroyer gave a lurch and he all but fell over the oilskinned rump of a rating bent double near the starboard torpedo-tubes.

'What the sod . . . ? Oh, it's you, is it, Ordinary Seaman Burden? Stand up straight for God's sake. Realize you nearly projected me into the drink, do you?'

'Sorry, Buff.' A round, good-humoured face grinned at Bustacle.

'Sorry's not good enough. What were you doing, praying?'

'Doing up my shoelace.'

'Best go and get your seaboots, lad. Bloody hell! This isn't the weather for white shoes.'

'Lost me seaboots. Someone's nicked 'em, Buff.'

Bustacle gave him a withering look. 'Useless article you are, eh? Can't look after your own essential gear. Ordinary Seaman Burden . . . and well named! Burden to yourself and the poor bloody ship.'

'Yes, Buff.'

'Glad you realize it.' Petty Officer Bustacle went on his way, reflecting on the slap-happy outlook of the hostilities-only ratings, of which the *Caithness* had plenty. Different from his own day . . . but you couldn't seriously criticize. They were all doing their bit and Burden wasn't much over nineteen years of age and facing danger and maybe death with that daft grin on his dial. . . .

iii

'Barometer's falling, sir,' Dawnay reported from behind Cameron's back. He added, 'Fast. Bottom's dropped out.'

'This is it then, Pilot?'

'I believe so, sir.'

Cameron pushed himself back at full arms' stretch from the forescreen, took another look all around through his binoculars. He was aware of the yeoman of signals also scanning the sea, though scarcely on the off-chance of picking up a visual signal. . . . Yeoman Venner's thin, cadaverous face was intent and strained as though he, too, were sharing Cameron's own feeling of being in limbo, cut off from all human contact beyond the ship herself. Then, a moment later, there came the first puff of wind: nothing much, but another indication. It soon went; the airlessness returned, feeling heavier than before. Then the wind came back with more assurance, playing around the decks. Aft at the peak, the White Ensign billowed out.

Dawnay caught Cameron's eye. Cameron said, 'First Lieutenant on the bridge, pronto.'

2

MAIN REACHED the bridge. 'You sent for me, sir?'

'Yes, Number One.' Cameron turned round. The rain had started now, coming with devastating suddenness to drop like solid water from the invisible sky. All hands were in Number Thirteens – white shorts and white short-sleeved shirts, or 'flannels' in the case of men dressed as seamen: by now it was too late for oilskins. All hands on the upper deck were soaked through already and would remain so until they came out the other side, except for one or two like Ordinary Seaman Burden who'd taken a precaution. Cameron said, 'Hurricane, and we're on its fringe. I'm going to alter to keep clear of the eye of the storm, but it could overtake us. See everything battened down, please, Number One.'

'Already in hand, sir.'

'Oh – well done! Saw it coming, did you?'

Main said, 'Yes, sir,' and felt grateful to Petty Officer Bustacle even though he refrained from mentioning the buffer's forethought.

'Carry on, then, Number One.'

Main went down the ladder, each movement spurting water as though he were a sponge. The wind was already on the increase and the seas were mounting. The destroyer wallowed badly, dipping her bows under to bring green sea cascading back as she lifted again. Solid water pounded down over the break of the fo'c'sle and swilled fast along the deck past the engineer's store and the torpedo-tubes, below the searchlight platform and Number Three gun above the splinter screen aft to drop back over the stern by the depth-charge throwers. It was by the charges that Main found Bustacle and said, 'Batten down, Petty Officer Bustacle.'

'Bridge, sir?'

'Yes.'

'Aye, aye, sir,' Bustacle said, straight-faced. The First Lieutenant went on his way, back for'ard the other side of the ship. He entered the seamen's messdeck and passed the order to the men off watch, shouted it down the hatch to the stokers' mess below. Mostly, precautions had been taken already by the leading hands, as soon as the destroyer had started reacting to the sea. Everything that could be secured – mess traps and tables, personal gear, movable equipment – was now firmed down against violent movement. At sea in what might be enemy waters the deadlights were always secured over the scuttles and few watertight doors remained open, just those essential to human movement. The word had gone from the forebridge to the engine-room that the ship was on the fringe of a hurricane and down below Mr Henty, warrant engineer, was supervising the preparations against bad weather. This he was doing from the starting platform, his personal equivalent of the bridge. There he would now remain until the weather moderated; no sleep or rest for the engineer in charge. So much could go wrong: right through the war, the destroyers, always in short supply, had been overworked and over-run, missing out on their proper peacetime dockyard maintenance, and it was up to their own engine-room staff to cope as best they could. But, like humans, ships didn't get any younger and over the last few months Mr Henty and his chief engine-room artificer, Tom Trigg, had had their work cut out to keep the old heap going at all, and God alone knew what a perishing hurricane might do. . . .

Dawnay and Cameron had huddled for a few moments beneath the canvas dodger that covered the chart table in the after part of the bridge and which, in the torrential downpour, might just as well have been uncovered. Dawnay made a small cross with a pencil. 'That's where I make the centre, sir. Hundred miles south-west of the Andamans, sixty miles south of our position.'

'Which by now is no more than dead reckoning.'

'Right. But not far out.'

Cameron nodded. Dawnay was a first-rate navigator; his dead reckoning was dependable within the normal limitations. Cameron had two choices open to him; he voiced them to Dawnay.

'We can head north, Pilot, and let it bypass us to the west as it makes towards the mouth of the Ganges.'

'Yes. . . .'

'Or we can cut across its northern fringe and hope to pass it before it comes north.'

'Make for Trinco – in other words, hold our course?' The destroyer, at the end of its patrol period, was in fact bound back for base.

'If the time factor's right, yes. Is it?'

Dawnay said, 'No, it's not. These things move fast, sir. We'd find ourselves up the creek without a paddle.'

'You're sure of that?'

'As sure as anyone can be, yes. It's all on the wrong quarter for us.'

Cameron pondered. To go north could bring them within the orbit of the Japanese operating out of Burma, out of the Gulf of Martaban and ports north, all of which were currently in Japanese occupation. Cameron was under orders merely to report sightings and not to engage unless forced to. The words 'unless forced to' gave him a certain scope but not much: the wishes of c-in-c East Indies Fleet had been clear enough. The Admiral wanted no avoidable losses . . . but a ship could be lost to a hurricane as easily and as finally as to the guns of the Japanese warships.

Cameron asked one more question. 'If we head north, have we a chance of standing clear?'

'A better one than if we hold our course, sir. The closer we keep towards Burma, the better the chance. But there's no guarantee on offer.'

'Right.' Cameron brought his head out from the canvas dodger. 'We head north, Pilot. Put her on course, please.'

'Aye, aye, sir.' Dawnay moved to the binnacle and passed the orders down the voice-pipe to the quartermaster in the wheelhouse below the bridge. 'Starboard ten.'

The disembodied repeat came back: 'Starboard ten, sir.' A brief pause, then: 'Ten of starboard wheel on, sir.'

'Midships . . . steady.'

'Midships, sir . . . wheel's amidships, sir . . . course oh oh five, sir.'

Dawnay said, 'Steer north.'

'Steer north, sir.'

Dawnay reported to Cameron. 'Course north, sir.'

'Thank you, Pilot. Engines to maximum revolutions.'

Dawnay passed the order down, direct to the starting platform via the sound-powered telephone. In the engine-room, where they had felt the effects of the heel as the destroyer came round to starboard, Mr Henty said, 'Jesus Christ on a motor-bike, in this? She'll never take it.' Everything was swaying and jerking as the destroyer rolled and pitched and it was the devil's own job for the warrant engineer to keep his feet at all. At his side CERA Trigg was more philosophic.

'She'll be all right.'

'Better be, Tom, or I'll be having someone's guts for garters, even if it's the skipper's.'

The revolutions were increased to full. There was a judder as the shafts spun faster and faster, increased engine sounds that didn't dim the crash and thunder of the seas on deck and along the thin steel sides of the engine spaces. In the boiler-room Leading Stoker Zebedee wiped cotton-waste across his streaming face as he watched the Stoker PO manipulate the valves that sent more oil fuel into the boilers to give a maximum head of steam to the engines. The deck itself seemed to shudder and vibrate, likewise the bulkheads. Zebedee didn't like it any more than Mr Henty did. But Leading Stoker Zebedee never did like anything in this life. Always disconsolate, was Zebedee, a tall, thin, gloomy man with a sniff and a permanent stoop, and when he remarked to the Stoker PO that the skipper must be bloody barmy, the Stoker PO's response was short.

'Shut up, Zebedee.'

Zebedee muttered something about jumped-up sods who knew bugger all – he was a good fifteen years older than the Stoker PO, being another of the RFR men. The Stoker PO didn't catch it, fortunately, since as Zebedee spoke an ERA 4 entered from the engine-room to report that the bridge had been on the phone with information. They were heading away from the hurricane's centre, going north, and doing it as fast as possible in case the hurricane was faster.

'Daft thing to say,' Zebedee said in an aggrieved voice. 'If the bugger's faster than us, then – '

'Shut up, Zebedee.'

'All very well,' Leading Stoker Zebedee persisted. 'What about the flaming Japs, eh? Japs are in the bloody Andamans, aren't they, and if we're going north we're going to come close to the Andamans. Burma and all.'

'That's what we joined for,' Stoker PO Tallis said. 'There's a war on – remember?'

'Get stuffed,' Zebedee said below his breath. That was what they'd all been saying for years ashore: *Don't you know there's a war on.* Like parrots – bloody civvies! Not so long ago it had been said once too often to Leading Stoker Zebedee when he'd been on leave and had gone out in plain clothes . . . he'd taken a pair of his wife's shoes to be re-soled and had complained when the man said they'd be a week. Before the war the job would have been done inside a couple

18

of days and Zebedee had said so. When he got the by this time customary response he'd lost his temper, leaned over the counter and grabbed the man by the scruff of the neck with the intention of filling him in. There had been a real shemozzle and another customer had run outside and then the police had come in the shape of a rotund constable who fortunately had been understanding when told that Zebedee was just back from escorting a Russian convoy. The constable had defused the situation and no action had been taken. It had been a close shave: if Zebedee had been done by the magistrates a report would have gone to his ship and he might have lost his rate. With a wife to support he needed the extra money, quite apart from the indignity of being back to plain stoker level. One thing about the Andrew, you stopped actual work once you got a leading hand's fouled anchor on your left sleeve: you supervised while the minions did the work. What work you did do was of a superior sort, needing brains. Mental work. Zebedee reckoned he had brains, all right, and currently he was employing them to decide that the skipper had made the wrong decision, taking the ship close to the Japs, or the Nips as the Americans called them. The Nips were right sods and best stood very well clear of. Zebedee would rather have faced a hurricane any day.

Up on deck, in the open air now filled with flying spray, the lifelines were being rigged fore and aft and the order had been passed by the bosun's mates that all hands not on watch were to keep off the upper deck. If – when – the weather worsened those on watch would simply stay there: it would be a case of watch on stop on. In hurricane conditions to venture up from below to relieve decks could be suicide; any man who went overboard would have to be left to drown, there were no two ways about that. Already the inessential men had been sent below; with the weather as it was, even the guns' crews were useless and had been withdrawn. The only personnel on deck now were those on the bridge: the Captain, the navigating officer, the officer of the watch, the yeoman of the watch, the messenger and the port and starboard lookouts. In the wheelhouse, the coxswain, Chief Petty Officer Chapman, was now on the wheel and with him were a relief QM and a telegraphsman. Leading Seaman Shiner White, the relief QM, was huddled in a corner, arms folded over a big beer gut, body wedged in firmly against the roll and heave of the destroyer. He was too fat to be moved far: there just wasn't the space. White had once overheard Ordinary Seaman Burden remarking that the killick gave the ship a list when he stayed too long in one spot. White had risked his hook by giving him a clip round the earhole. It didn't do, to let ordinary seamen get away with cheek. Once the rot set in, you'd had it.

CPO Chapman, senior rating of the lower deck, a kind of regimental sergeant-major without a warrant, kept his eyes on the gyro repeater in front of him as he steadied himself against the roll by keeping his feet well apart. He was aware that the ship's safety depended firstly on the skipper giving the right orders and secondly on himself carrying them out with precision. A degree or two either way, a moment's inattention, and they could broach to. If the ship came across the wind and sea, brought broadside on, they would wallow in the troughs in danger of being submerged by the falling wave-crests. Chapman was prepared to admit a third to join him and the skipper, to make a vital triumvirate, or trinity: Mr Henty, warrant engineer. If the engines failed, that too would mean the end. Engines had their uses even though Chapman didn't like them. A fleet reservist, CPO Chapman was elderly to be still at sea in wartime and his naval recollections went back to the days of the *Dreadnought*, in which he'd served as boy second class, a nipper of fourteen living in a teeming broadside mess right against the barbette guns with water slopping in through the gun-ports when the battleship rolled in a heavy sea. . . . *Dreadnought* had been the first sizeable warship to be equipped with turbine engines, and the stokers had boasted about this, Chapman remembered. Even so, those early days hadn't been so far removed from the old sailing navy, in which Bill Chapman's grandfather had served as a seaman petty officer second class. His grandfather had been an old man full of sailors' yarns and the young Chapman had learned a lot from him and had been given a nostalgia for days he himself had never known.

With the coming of steam it had been all dirt and stink. Chapman remembered days spent coaling ships, in home ports, in Gibraltar, Port Said, Aden, Singapore . . . coal-dust everywhere, and the ship to be cleaned down the moment the evolution was complete. Cleaned down from truck to waterline outside, and every space below decks, for coal-dust had an extraordinarily penetrative quality and battleships' executive officers were always pernickety men. Chapman had been glad enough to see the passing of coal in favour of oil firing. One up to Winston Churchill, right back in the last lot . . . First Lord of the Admiralty, with foresight.

By now the destroyer was groaning, as if in pain, creaking in all her elderly joints and plates, an old woman with arthritis. Chapman's hands were steady on the wheel, tending her through, meeting each lurch of the ship's head, keeping her as exactly as possible on course. He believed that even now they were only on the fringe of the storm, and he felt in his bones that they were in for something extra special.

Chapman was aware of Leading Seaman White in his corner. That gut, and a big red face, with many chins – Shiner White was no chicken either, yet another RFR man. And not entirely surprisingly, for Shiner White had the ability to nod off anywhere at any time, he was asleep, head drooped sideways and a stream of saliva running down his chins from the corner of his mouth. Chapman had an urge to stick a pin in Shiner's gut and see it collapse inwards like a barrage balloon caught by flak.

iii

The wind was strong enough to take the breath away, up there on the forebridge. Cameron found he had to face sideways, away from the full force. In point of fact there was nothing for him to do currently, nothing for anyone to do other than hold the ship on course and keep as good a lookout as was possible in visibility that wasn't far off nil. The radar was getting echoes off the massive waves, might not isolate another vessel. It was up to God rather than himself, Cameron reflected – or luck, if you weren't religious. Thinking of God, Cameron turned to glance at Pegram, the RNVR lieutenant currently in charge of the watch.

Their eyes met. There was a curious confidence about John Pegram which Cameron found reassuring, since Pegram was said to be in close touch with the Almighty. Cameron grinned at him, moved aft and put his lips close to his ear. 'Any signals from aloft?' he asked. Pegram never minded being twitted, his faith was strong enough to ride it, and he was a good-humoured man.

'Strict w/T silence being maintained, sir,' he answered.

'I see. Let me know of any transmission, won't you?'

'I will, sir.' Pegram paused. 'There's one thing, sir.'

'Yes?'

'I may have said this before . . . but I've always had a very strong feeling I'm going to come through the war. That holds good now. And that means – '

'Good news for us all. Let's hope you're right, old chap. Keep on the wavelength!' Cameron moved back to his position in the fore part of the bridge. He watched out ahead, his mind roving over the course of the war in the east, over the relentless advance of the Japanese forces north from Singapore, a long line of unbroken success ever since Singapore had fallen in 1942. The advance on Burma, the grip on Malaya, the Dutch East Indies, New Guinea, their domination of the Bay of Bengal which made every patrol potentially a time of the utmost danger. The holding of General Slim's Fourteenth Army, the forgotten army as they called themselves, south of Mandalay, bogging them down in the horror of the jungle swamps and inhibiting any drive down the Irrawaddy towards Rangoon. The Japanese seemed unconquerable; there were so many of them and they were all fanatical, as Captain Anderson had said back in Trinco, for

Nihon-koku Tenno Hirohito, their Emperor, a god in his own divine right. But one day a time might come; it would have to. The Japs could not be allowed to dominate the far east. And certainly the Americans at least were determined that they would not.

Behind Cameron, holding fast to the binnacle, Lieutenant Pegram, as the wind's noise rose to a shriek, sent up a brief and pointed prayer. *Please God, save our souls this day.* Pegram, in fact, believed that God would do just that in any case, but it didn't pay to take too much for granted: you had to put in the actual request. It was a matter of politeness, of good manners, as much as anything else. John Pegram, while at Cambridge, had toyed with the idea of entering the ministry and might have done so had the war not intervened. But to have in a sense opted out of the fighting after 3 September 1939 had happened would have seemed to him the easy way, an act of cowardice, and as such by no means to be approved by God. Once the war was over, then he might think again. Whatever he did with his life it would have to be something basic; and by basic he meant the real callings such as the sea or farming and the real, meaningful professions such as medicine and the Church, the one caring for the body on earth and the other for the spirit both on earth and afterwards. Anything else was frippery, the icing on the cake. Accountants, lawyers, engineers, politicians, finance wizards, company directors, anything you cared to name – there was nothing basic about any of them. They could at a pinch, and Pegram admitted the pinch, be done without.

The navigator had now moved alongside Cameron in the fore part of the bridge. Pegram looked at him: his face was more or less expressionless but Pegram believed he detected anxiety. Dawnay, of course, knew this part of the world but the hurricanes he had faced in the past would have been from the greater security of a very much bigger ship than the *Caithness*, which was of only some 1700 tons displacement. The BI liners – Pegram made a guess – were mostly around 8000 to 10,000 tons, a different kettle of fish. Small ships

23

could probably be submerged by the huge waves blown up by a hurricane, where the wind could scream at well over a hundred knots. That might be in Dawnay's mind. A pity, Pegram thought, that the Pilot hadn't faith – he knew he hadn't because he'd said so more than once. According to Dawnay, there was a scientific explanation for everything in the universe and anything spiritual was bunk.

As Pegram watched, Cameron moved alongside him to speak down the voice-pipe to the wheelhouse.

'Cox'n – '

'Sir?'

'Call up damage control, Cox'n. I'd like a report.'

'Aye, aye, sir, right away.' In the wheelhouse CPO Chapman spoke to the telegraphsman. 'You, Flatt. Call up the First Lieutenant in damage control, ask him how's his father.'

'Eh?' Ordinary Seaman Flatt looked astonished. 'Don't get it, Chief – '

'Use your loaf, lad. Skipper wants a report.'

'Oh.' Flatt lurched across the wheelhouse and blew down a voice-pipe that connected with the central point of the damage-control parties, which happened to be the tiller flat right aft. Main answered himself and Flatt passed his message. 'Skipper, sir, wants a report.'

'Everything under control,' came Main's voice, hollow and metallic. 'Who's that?'

'Flatt, sir.'

'Ah. Well, Flatt, Lieutenant-Commander Cameron is not the skipper to you. He's the Captain. Understood?'

'Yessir. Sorry, sir.' Flatt, flustered now, almost saluted down the voice-pipe. He heard the slam of the plug going back in at the other end and reported to the coxswain. 'First Lieutenant says, everything under control.'

'Right you are, lad.' Chapman passed the message up and spared a thought for the men down there in the tiller flat, a nasty little compartment right in the stern of the ship, slap over the rudder, the place where you could steer from as a last resort if the bridge or the telemotor steering gear packed up – steer by pulley-hauley, with tackles on the rudder post itself, and bloody hard work it could be. He hoped he never had to do it.

In the tiller flat itself Main was listening to the thunder of the sea all around him, plus the clatter from the steering engine every time the coxswain turned the wheel up topsides. He felt as if he were in a sound-box: everything drummed and rattled so much that he could scarcely think. The sea dropping down from for'ard, and dropping right overhead as well when solid water came over the depth-charge racks and throwers and pushed the stern down momentarily each time; the sea battering at the destroyer's thin steel sides and beneath him the terrible racket from the screws whenever the ship went the other way and dipped its head under and the screws, coming clear of the water's grip, raced dangerously. Main felt claustrophobic in the tiller flat, no room to swing a cat and a very low deckhead that seemed about to press down on him and squash him. Once, aboard a cruiser, he'd been in a watertight compartment right above the double bottoms, a compartment used for the stowage of the confidential books and recyphering and recoding tables, when someone, not knowing anyone was below – or possibly as a particularly nasty kind of practical joke – had shut the hatch above him. It was a heavy hatch cover with a counterbalancing weight and once the clips were on up top there was no way of opening it from below. Main had never forgotten the sense of panic: he might not have been missed for hours, he was at that time a relatively unimportant sub-lieutenant, and the air wouldn't have lasted long. The relief when the hatch was opened, apparently without human agency – which gave credence to the practical-joke theory – had been like a second birth. If Main had ever identified the joker, he would have murdered him. Anyway, the experience lingered on. It was partly that and partly the close atmosphere that was making him sweat now: he was sticky all over and his face was streaming. ERA

25

Walsh, the engine-room rating attached to damage control, noticed it and commented.

'Feeling the heat, sir?'

'Yes.' Main dabbed with a handkerchief.

'It's a real bugger down here, sir. Enough to cook a goose.'

Main said, 'We won't talk about cooked geese, Walsh, if you don't mind.'

'Sorry, sir.' Walsh gave a grin that faded under the look on Jimmy's face. Maybe Jimmy was superstitious or something . . . but superstitious or not, Walsh had heard from the seamen ratings that Jimmy was a prickly sod and you had to watch your step. Right now Jimmy was looking edgy. Walsh hoped he knew what to do in an emergency. He didn't know it but Main was hoping the same thing. Main had no experience of damage control, or only a smattering of the general principles. In a ship carrying engineer officers, the job would have gone to one of them. Aboard the *Caithness*, with just Mr Henty, warrant engineer, the first requirement was the engines themselves. Main, in general charge, would not necessarily be confined to the tiller flat: if something should happen elsewhere, say if a giant wave twisted the fo'c'sle plating, or ripped out Number One or Number Two gun and left a hole for the seas to flood down into the messdecks . . . well, he would have to make his way for'ard along the half-submerged deck and take charge there. He didn't relish the prospect at all. It would really be an impossible situation; in attempting to plug anything against the inrush of water, someone was going to be washed overboard for sure. It would have to be done from below, but how? Main thought hard about shoring-up beams, chocks, cement boxes, collision mats, even lashed hammocks for stuffing into split seams. It was as well to be mentally prepared.

iv

No one was was prepared for what did happen some hours later. Fortunately it was not of itself a threat to the ship but it left behind it a feeling of horror and foreboding: it was the yeoman of signals who saw it first and yelled a warning to the Captain.

'Boat, sir, dead ahead! Looks like a lifeboat, sir!'

Cameron saw it and reacted in the same instant. 'Starboard ten,' he called to Pegram. Pegram passed the order down; the ship's head swung as the wheel went over in Chapman's steady hands. They all held their breath: this was the moment of danger, the moment when the wind would be brought closer abeam and they could roll over: that wind was now gusting to ninety knots. In the wheelhouse Chapman gripped the wheel hard and found the sweat running like a river; in the tiller flat the damage-control parties felt the alteration, the reacting as the stern swept round and the angle of roll increased wickedly. From the open bridge Cameron and Dawnay saw the lifeboat veer away to port, moving apparently to safety, and then as Cameron brought the ship back on course they saw it lifted by a great-grandfather of a sea, lifted high to be flung clear across the destroyer's bows and be crashed down into a trough to vanish as suddenly as it had appeared. But as it passed across the fo'c'sle plating and the guns and the anchors it had left its dropping like a seagull over Ailsa Craig: a body, falling to the deck to fetch up across the starboard cable, where it remained wedged against the rushing torrent, held fast with a leg caught by some miracle beneath the heavy links of the cable itself.

Cameron looked down through his binoculars, glimpsing the body now and again as the water drained away. 'Small,' he said. 'And Jap. Probably, almost certainly, dead. But we're going to have to make sure.'

3

'IT'LL BE bloody dangerous,' Cameron said.

'Not dangerous,' Dawnay said briefly. 'Suicidal. Does a Jap matter that much, sir?'

'If he's alive, he may have information . . . disposition of enemy forces. It's our job to collect intelligence, Pilot.'

'But he can't possibly be alive!'

'I think he is,' Cameron said. 'I believe I saw a movement of his hand.' A moment later Dawnay saw it too: the hand that had grasped the cable, self-preservative against the pounding sea and the destroyer's roll. That roll had eased now that Cameron had brought the ship's head back into the wind and sea, but the weather conditions on the fo'c'sle were as bad as ever if not worse: the wind felt even stronger. Someone had to go out there: Cameron steeled himself to give the order. He wished he could go himself rather than give it: he hated giving any order that he could not perform himself, but the Captain had no right to risk depriving his ship's company of his services with the ship itself in danger.

It was John Pegram who came to his rescue. Pegram said. 'I'll go, sir. I'll be all right. I know that.'

Cameron nodded, remembering what Pegram had said earlier. 'Thank you for that, Pegram. You'll need assistance – two hands.' He stepped to the wheelhouse voice-pipe. 'Cox'n – messenger to Petty Officer Tucker – I believe he's in the seamen's messdeck. Two men, volunteers for preference, to go for'ard with Mr Pegram and collect a Jap from the fo'c'sle.' He heard the astonished reaction up the voice-pipe: the wheelhouse, with the ship battened down and all deadlights closed, had no view of the deck. Briefly he explained, and added, 'Inform the Surgeon Lieutenant. I'll have the man sent aft to the wardroom flat.'

ii

When the message reached Surgeon Lieutenant Styles in the wardroom, where he had wedged himself deep into a leather armchair and was reading an ancient copy of *London Opinion*, he at once became the first volunteer to accompany Pegram. It was, he said, his duty as a doctor to attend the injured on the spot if possible. The man would most likely need a pain-killing injection. Styles sent a message back to the bridge to this effect and then after contacting his sick-berth attendant left the security of the wardroom for the horrible struggle along the upper deck, clinging fast to the lifeline with one hand while the other clutched the bag prepared for him by the SBA. The wind took his breath away, the swirling water lifted him off his legs and soaked him through his oilskin within two seconds flat. But Styles didn't give that a thought: Styles was tough and a keep-fit fanatic. He'd done his student years at Guy's and was almost automatically a rugger player; and he had a strong sense of duty before self. He was faced with a challenge and he would meet it in the best traditions of his Hippocratic oath. With difficulty he reached the battened-down door into the galley flat, off which led the seamen's messdeck where he was to pick up the second volunteer; he found that this was Petty Officer Tucker in person. Like the Captain, Tucker didn't like asking men to do what he didn't do himself and in his case he had the advantage over the skipper: there was only one skipper but they had plenty of petty officers. So he was going. Pegram was waiting with him now, the watch on the bridge having been taken over by Dawnay.

Pegram said, 'Well, we won't waste time. Port ladder to the break of the fo'c'sle, Doc. Watch it when we come out of the lee of the bridge at the head of the ladder. Just hold on tight – and don't lose your bag of tricks.'

Styles grinned and flexed his fingers. 'Don't worry,' he said. His hands were like spades, each finger a Cumberland sausage: the sheer size had determined his course for medicine pure and simple rather than surgery. A scalpel would simply have got lost.

Pegram said, 'The Old Man wants him alive if possible.'

Styles asked rhetorically, 'What d'you imagine I want? I'm a medico and I don't like losing patients.'

'Sorry I spoke!' Pegram grinned, and nodded at Tucker. 'Right, PO, open up and away we go.' Then he thought of something else. 'What about carrying him back?'

'Neil Robertson stretcher,' Styles said. 'My SBA's bringing one, any minute now. Just hold on a tick.' As he spoke, the clips began coming off the door to the upper deck and the SBA was seen, his face as white as paper and his eyes dead scared, a Neil Robertson stretcher lashed to his back with a length of codline.

Tucker said, 'Stay where you are, lad, we're all coming out now.' He stepped through into the wind's strength, his oilskin flattened to the front of his body and billowing out behind like a black tent. He held the door open until the others were through, then slammed it shut and quickly put on the clips. Tucker looked confident, almost nonchalant, because as a PO and captain of the fo'c'sle he had to, no option. But inside he was as scared as the SBA. Tucker had done plenty of sea-time, before the war and during it, and he'd seen plenty of accidents happen. In weather like this it was always a case of one missed handhold and you were away, over the side and goodbye all. He'd seen wires part and, in springing back, take off arms or legs like a butcher's cleaver, or spill a man's stomach out on the deck, gutting him like a herring. He'd seen men crushed by anchor-cables before now, when ranging cable in a dry dock and one of the slips went and the great links bounded free, coming out of the navel pipe like an express train from a tunnel. But of course you didn't dwell on such things, you just got on with the job and put your trust in the two divinities, God and the skipper. So now Tucker got on with it, taking personal charge of the terrified SBA and chivvying him up the port ladder with a steadying hand and words of encouragement.

'Not a poultice walloper's job, lad, is it, but never mind, we'll make a seaman of you yet, you bet your life. Steady now – whoops-a-daisy! Nothing in it so long as you hold on, is there, eh?' Behind Pegram they got their feet on the fo'c'sle plating and began the struggle into the teeth of the wind past Numbers One and Two guns, the 4.7s. Up there it was nothing short of murderous and each step into the wind took an age. It was like trying to push through a watertight door, Tucker thought, clipped down hard and unyielding. With the wind came the sea, battering them to a standstill until the water swept past and they could make a little more progress. Tucker was aware of Cameron staring down from the forebridge and looking anguished: skippers throughout the centuries of seafaring had always faced enormous responsibilities for life and death and most of them were human inside. Tucker struggled on towards the Japanese, still nipped by the cable, a hand still grasping for safety, a hand that could be in a death-grasp, unmoving for all Tucker could yet say. Maybe they would have to break it clear in order to remove the body, if there was any point in removing a dead body – but then of course you couldn't face a hurricane with bad luck left on the fo'c'sle. Too grisly, and seamen were by and large superstitious folk and disliked going to sea with corpses, though there had been times enough in this war when they hadn't been able to get the dead out from the shatter and twist of turrets and bulkheads that had taken a projy.

This one, however, wasn't dead.

When at last they reached the Japanese, Styles rolled back an eyelid and felt for a pulse. Then, holding on himself to the cable, he felt carefully around the limbs and lifted the head.

31

There was blood at the back of the head and both legs and an arm were broken, multiple fractures. Styles fumbled around in his bag and brought out a ready-filled hypodermic. No time for the niceties now, no point in sterilizing the point of insertion, not with the sea sweeping over continually. He aimed for a muscle and jabbed and squeezed then he shouted into the SBA's ear to get the stretcher laid out. With Pegram and Tucker helping, the unconscious man was freed from the cable that had been his salvation and lifted on to the Neil Robertson stretcher and strapped firmly in. No time lost now, Styles gave the word and the stretcher was lifted and the move back to the break of the fo'c'sle began. With the wind behind them, screaming like a devil's orchestra, battering at the oilskins, they almost took off into the air. They kept low, close to the deck, offering as little wind resistance as possible, hands grabbing for the cable and the slips and the cable-holders and centre-line capstan, guardrails, gun-barrels, anything to hold them from becoming airborne. Pegram went first down the ladder and steadied the bulky stretcher from below while Tucker and the SBA tended it over the head of the ladder and started down behind it. That was when things went wrong. Petty Officer Tucker's seaboot slid away from the top rung and he crashed headlong. The SBA failed to hold the stretcher; Styles was too late with his grab. The stretcher shot down the ladder, knocking Pegram off his grip on the handrail. He fetched up with his body curled round one of the guardrail stanchions, looking down into sea that rose to submerge him until he struggled back to safety.

The stretcher had jammed itself a little farther aft along the deck, one of the straps caught on a clip of the door into the engineer's store. The Jap, Styles thought as he slid down the ladder, was certainly meant to survive. The SBA was clinging to the foot of the ladder, his mouth open like a fish and his face whiter than ever.

Styles asked, looking around, 'Where's the PO?'

No one knew. Then they saw him: an oilskinned body in the grip of a huge wave, flinging inwards from the port beam, moving very fast to impact against the guardrail of the searchlight platform amidships. He dropped to the deck below, a formless mass that was at once picked up by a sea tumbling down from the break of the fo'c'sle and washed aft to vanish back into the water beneath the port guardrail aft of the torpedo-tubes.

He wasn't seen again.

iii

In the wheelhouse Chapman said, 'Skipper'll take it hard, I reckon. There's some who'll say . . . look, Shiner. What's your first thought, eh?'

Leading Seaman White sucked at a hollow tooth. 'Why waste a good matlow on a fornicating Jap?'

Chapman nodded. 'Yes. But if you stop to think about it – '

'Japs are 'uman same as us?'

Chapman said with a grin, 'I wouldn't go so far as that. No – it's just that it was his duty. Skipper had no choice. Little yellow bugger'll be made to talk.'

'Japs don't talk, so I've 'eard, 'Swain.'

Chapman offered no further comment. What White had said was probably true, the Japs were a cussed lot and believed themselves to be the Lord's anointed, superior to everyone else on earth, and much dedicated to the warrior concept and personal honour. All the same, there were always ways and means. And that Jap, and the lifeboat he'd dropped from, had to have come from somewhere, some ship – one that had maybe foundered in the same hurricane that the *Caithness* was currently facing. It might be of some help to the war effort in the Bay of Bengal and the Indian Ocean to find out what the ship was, what she was doing, where from and where to, all that sort of thing. But there would be plenty on the messdecks who would mutter about priorities; Tucker had been a first-rate PO and a popular one too, always fair, and lenient on inexperience – which couldn't be said of all petty officers. Green was a colour that made many a PO see red.

Above on the bridge, somewhat similar thoughts were running through Cameron's mind. He dismissed them as an irrelevance, while far from dismissing Tucker himself. Tucker, a married man with three children, was going to be missed aboard as well as in Pompey, and in any case Cameron always felt casualties keenly. But a duty had been done and there was nothing to be gained by morbidity. The future was still there, the ship was still at much risk, the war had to be fought on. A captain's mind must be clear. And they had the Jap alive. . . .

Cameron used the voice-pipe once again. 'Cox'n . . . call the wardroom, ask the doctor what the score is now, all right?'

'Aye, aye, sir.' Chapman passed the order to Ordinary Seaman Flatt. In the wardroom – used in action as an emergency dressing station and now in use to accommodate the Japanese prisoner because the tiny sick bay already had an injured rating in it – Styles answered. The report went back to the bridge that the man was still unconscious, would have to be kept doped for quite a while after regaining consciousness, and it was as yet early days to say whether or not he would pull through or when he would be fit to be questioned, assuming he did pull through.

'He'd better not die on us,' Cameron said to Dawnay, and Dawnay nodded understandingly. A dead Jap for a dead PO would be a poor exchange. But that was in the doctor's hands and meanwhile there were more immediate anxieties. Dawnay hadn't thought the wind could increase much more; but it had. It was likely the storm was moving faster than expected and was overtaking them, in which case it was going to be touch and go for them all. Dawnay glanced at the midshipman, now on watch in Pegram's place. Pegram, once below, had been told to stay there, send up a relief and take the opportunity to snatch some sleep himself. And the midshipman, his inexperience not mattering much with the Captain and the navigator on the bridge with him, was showing distinct signs of unease. Midshipman Tillotson was

RNR like Dawnay, but he had never actually been to sea in peacetime and not much since the outbreak of war: three months earlier, he had been fresh from the nautical college at Pangbourne. He was now facing his very first bad weather.

'Chin up,' Dawnay shouted briefly.

'Yes, sir. I'm all right, sir.'

'Good lad.' Dawnay gripped his shoulder. 'When the war's over, apply for a berth in BI. You can tell 'em you've been here before!'

Tillotson responded with a somewhat shaky grin. He wasn't sea material and had no intention of remaining at sea after the war. Dawnay, having yarned with him from time to time, knew this. The Pangbourne cadets had the choice of sitting the examination for special entry to the RN, or of applying for an attenuated apprenticeship in the Merchant Service; but, although most did in fact go to sea one way or the other, they had other options as well. They were not forced to the sea life and some chose other and very different professions. Midshipman Tillotson had decided he wanted to chuck the sea idea and become a vet. However, it was wartime and he had been automatically projected into the role of midshipman RNR and that, for now, was that. The horses and cattle, or alternatively the poodles and lapdogs of rich old ladies, would have to wait. In the meantime Midshipman Tillotson spent a good deal of his time day-dreaming about a happier future and trying to make up his mind whether he was more cut out to be a vet in farming country – all hard work and calf delivery, not much wealth but a good deal of satisfaction – or a town vet growing fat on overfed pets.

Dawnay knew this too. Dawnay, a seaman to his fingertips, had had his own choice to make: the glamour of the liners, the deadly routine of the North Atlantic and its rich passenger trade, or the cargo-liners where you could be a seaman and not part a lounge lizard. For him the choice had been dead easy, since he had a natural aversion to passengers. Cargo couldn't argue, couldn't make complaints about bugger-all

35

like passengers . . . now, he saw that Tillotson's mind was far away and he gave him a sharp reminder.

'Watch that gyro repeater, Mid. Don't take your eyes off it. Forget the pampered pussies, all right? You're the officer of the watch. Don't forget it.'

In the wheelhouse, the navigator's words had penetrated via the voice-pipe and had been picked up by Shiner White, who was about to relieve CPO Chapman for a spell on the wheel. White said, "Know what, 'Swain?'

'What?'

'Wouldn't mind pampering a pussy right now. . . .'

'At your age, Leading Seaman White?' Chapman clicked his tongue in mock disapproval. 'Lift your thoughts above your belt, can't you, eh?'

'Not often,' White said.

Chapman asked formal permission from the bridge to hand over, then sank down into the corner just vacated by White. It was uncomfortable but it was something to be off his feet for a while. He was getting a shade elderly for this kind of lark; slippers and a nice coal fire, and a cup of tea, were more in his line these days. Though at first, back in September 1939, or a few weeks before that date in fact, he'd been glad enough to be called back to the Andrew, see the inside of Pompey barracks again and renew old friendships with men drawn back from all corners of the British Isles to serve again at sea. It had been so easy to drop back into the old routine, nostalgic to hear the Tannoy issuing orders around the blocks and across the parade ground . . . Both Watches of the Hands Fall In, Stand Easy, Out Pipes, Hands to Dinner. It had made Chapman feel younger to begin with, made him feel an up-and-coming young leading seaman again . . . there had even been a certain nostalgia in being re-entered on the navy's books as an able seaman on first reporting, and then next day advanced to his pensioner rate of chief petty officer, the reason for all this being that if he'd been entered as Chief PO then come what may he could never have been disrated. Their Lordships of the Admiralty would never rest easy in their gilded beds if they had lost the sanction of disrating anyone who transgressed, and even a CPO could do that. Early nostalgia: now the nostalgia, after so many years of war and continual sea-time, had gone the other way and Chapman's thoughts were of home.

Home and the missus, in Fareham, not far from Pompey.

The missus worried about him. She didn't often say so, but he knew she did. It came through in her letters – she wrote nearly every day, and whenever the mail caught up with the ship Chapman had enough reading matter to last a fortnight – and it came through in the set of her face when he was on leave, especially the last night of the leave. All wives worried, of course they did, so did mothers, but none so sorely as Win. Having no kids was probably the reason: he was all she'd got and if he went her world would collapse.

His recall had hit Win hard. Of course, like everyone else after Neville Chamberlain had come back the year before from Munich, waving his umbrella and talking about peace in our time, Win had seen it coming. Chamberlain had seemed to think that Herr Hitler was a good bloke, reasonable, with no more territorial demands to make, but everyone else, Win Chapman included, had known different. Hitler was a monster with red claws dipped in blood and he wouldn't be turned from his desire to conquer Britain. Win had gone through the whole of that next year looking sort of haunted, and there had been long silences while she stared into the winter fire in the parlour in Fareham and studied Bill's face when she thought he was unaware. When at last the blow had fallen, when his call-up papers had come and the Anderson shelters were being built in Pompey, all ready for the air raids, she had put on a show of stiff upper lip and all that, but he knew what was going on inside.

Chapman shifted his bottom on the steel deck of the wheelhouse and thought it was just as well they didn't get the Bay of Bengal weather reports back across the sea in Fareham. . . . He looked up at Shiner White, handling the wheel as competently as Chapman did himself, though the

37

moment things got really tricky he would be taking the ship again on orders from the bridge. He reflected on White: married like himself, but a very different sort. White was said to be one of the traditional Jack Tars, the wife in every port sort; that was as maybe, but Chapman did know for sure that he had the biggest collection of blue photographs that he'd ever known aboard any of His Majesty's ships. Port Said had always been a fruitful warehouse of dirty postcards and that, so was Aden, and plenty of other places east of Suez. Shiner White was a connoisseur in that direction; his fame was almost legendary. He didn't, Chapman would have thought, have much personal glamour: that big gut, several chins, and scarcely ever changed his socks.

A good seaman, though.

Good and ready.

When the daddy of all waves took the *Caithness*, took her suddenly, with no warning, Shiner White had already braced his muscles in the right direction for the order when it came down the voice-pipe in a high shout from Midshipman Tillotson.

'*Hard-a-starboard!*'

'Hard-a-starboard, sir.' The wheel was half-way there almost before the midshipman's order was complete. 'Wheel's hard-a-starboard, sir.'

Chapman, on his feet, lurching as the deck heeled violently, took over and reported: 'Cox'n on the wheel, sir!'

'Thank you, Cox'n,' Tillotson said up above.

Chapman held the wheel hard over and started praying. He didn't like the feel of the ship, too soggy, too sluggish, and wallowing now like a sick porpoise. He believed they had broached to. If they had, they might never be able to turn her head back into the wind and sea. There were crashings and bangings from below – some of the messdeck gear evidently hadn't been all that well secured against the weather. The sound of the wind had gone, and that was ominous. It was still blowing – it had to be unless they'd reached the eye of the storm and had passed suddenly from gale to windlessness,

38

and Chapman didn't reckon it could be that or the skipper wouldn't still be holding her on full starboard wheel.

It was White who said it. 'Fallen off, 'Swain. In the trough.'

'Reckon that's right.'

'We going to be all right, Chief?' This was Ordinary Seaman Flatt.

'We'll be all right, lad,' Chapman said. They might, if God so decided. It was up to him now. Him and the skipper . . . they must be deep in the trough, great walls of water lifting to either beam, so high that the crests were deflecting the wind right above their heads. It wouldn't last; it couldn't. Soon another wave would sweep beneath them, and lift them, twisting like a toy boat in a fast-flowing river, back to the gale-torn heights, and which way they would be pointing then, Chapman didn't know. Seconds passed like centuries. More sounds, sounds of foreboding, came from aft – could be, Chapman thought, from the engine-room or boiler-room.

Then, at last, the order came, this time Dawnay's voice.

'Midships!'

'Midships, sir.' The wheel spun back, running through Chapman's hands. 'Wheel's amidships, sir.'

'Steady.'

'Steady, sir. Course one eight oh, sir.'

They'd turned a half circle, on to the reciprocal of their previous course. There was nothing further from the bridge: the next thing that came down the voice-pipe was water that spurted drenchingly over the coxswain, and then came the lurch, the heave followed by what felt like a headlong dive. As Chapman had forecast, something big had swept beneath them. The effect was felt alarmingly in the engine spaces aft: Mr Henty grabbed for a handhold as his feet shot from under him on the oily, slippery starting platform, and Chief ERA Trigg was hurtled against a bank of dials and gauges, badly bruising his left shoulder. He resumed his feet with an oath. Glass smashed, falling to the deck. There was a shrieking sound from the spinning main shafts as the screws bit into nothing more solid than air. The destroyer's after part shook, like a cow's tail, seeming to detach from the rest of the hull – that was how Mr Henty put it to himself. Then he too, like Chapman in the wheelhouse, felt the diving sensation and concluded that they were sliding down the side of a mountainous wave, just as though they were tobogganing down a winter hillside.

In the wardroom there was something like total chaos but Styles and the SBA had managed to salvage their patient, who was already strapped down on the settee that ran along the side below the row of deadlight-shrouded scuttles. They just knelt on him; it might not do him much good but it was better than allowing him to be thrown across the wardroom if the strapping should fail to take the strain. They knelt, and they held on to the butterfly screws of the deadlights as the side of the wardroom lifted.

'She's going to turn over!' The SBA was shaking badly.

Styles said nothing. He was no seaman any more than his SBA, and turn over, he believed, they well might. It certainly felt like it. If they did, there was a naval nursing sister in Haslar hospital near Portsmouth who was going to miss the current light of her life until a replacement came along with the next intake from the medical schools. Surgeon Lieutenant Styles saw no way anyone could come out if the ship turned turtle and though some might live for a while in a pocket of air and manage to find a way out, they wouldn't last two minutes after coming to the surface. Not in weather like this.

iv

The discomfort in the tiller flat was about the worst any of the men down there had ever known. A filthy cold fug and the compartment being flung about like a tin can all on its own, being kicked along the street by an urchin. Each time the screws did their racing act it was like being hit by a sledgehammer; and the sheer noise was appalling, deafening, making the head reel and constructive thought hard to come by. What made it much worse was Sub-Lieutenant Hanson's lack of sea-legs: Hanson, a recently-promoted RNVR ex-lower deck, had never got accustomed to the sea's motion and now he was being violently sick all over the place, the only one of the damage-control parties to be so affected.

Edgily Main said, 'For God's sake! Aren't you emptied out yet, Sub?'

The only response was a groan and an attempted remark that ended in the upsurge of more green bile – Hanson's stomach was indeed empty of all but that, and of that there seemed to be an endless supply. And it was not possible, in the very restricted space of the tiller flat, to stand clear of the source; the result was inevitable and all present were suffering equally. The stench was murderous. But much worse than smell and discomfort was the knowledge that the ship was in real danger; her riveted seams could stand so much and no more. A point would come, must come if the hurricane didn't release her from its grip, when she would surrender to the pounding and die. Rivets would be sprung, and seams would open to the water. The First Lieutenant with his damage-control parties might be able to plug the leaks but once seams started to go they tended to keep on going, the rivets springing out like dropped stitches in a piece of knitting. It was Able Seaman Gizzard, a three-badgeman known to the ship's company as Stripey, who first noticed – whilst surreptitiously eating a bar of Cadbury's chocolate from the canteen – that the process seemed to be beginning in the tiller flat itelf. A trickle of water was seeping from a rivet and to Gizzard's eyes it looked as though the plates were moving apart – not much, certainly, but enough to give anyone down there the runs.

At once, Gizzard broke off from eating and reported to the First Lieutenant. 'Aft there, sir! See it, do you, sir?'

Main saw it all right. There was a constant drip and the plates did appear to be shifting – that could be seen from the line where the grey paint ended. Main called the wheelhouse, pronto. Chief PO Chapman made the report to the bridge, his tone expressionless but the words foreboding: 'First

Lieutenant, sir, reports tiller flat making water. Seam opening, sir.'

'What's he doing about it, Cox'n?'

'Trying to plug, sir.'

'Thank you, Cox'n. Pass to the tiller flat, I'm to be kept informed. But if anything goes suddenly, the tiller flat's to be abandoned and battened down without further orders.' Cameron caught Dawnay's eye. He said. 'That's all we needed, Pilot!'

Caithness staggered on, her White Ensign bar taut as it flew from the gaff, her decks awash so that she looked like a half-submerged submarine, taking hammer-blow after hammer-blow from the wind's force and the battering sea. In the tiller flat they were doing all that could be done, which wasn't much. This was no occasion for shoring beams: they could only plug, using tar and oakum and strips of canvas, little more than a cosmetic operation that would have no effect whatsoever if the seam widened when more rivets went. Main knew it would be up to him to recognize, and recognize instantly, when the moment had come to order all hands out. If the seam went finally, it would go with a rush and the water would flood in, knocking them all off their feet and filling the compartment to the hatch in seconds. Main sweated: he had to fight down his instinctive urge to abandon now, while there was time. But he had a duty not to be precipitate: with him in the tiller flat was Petty Officer Kennet, the quarterdeck division's PO. Kennet's eye was on him and there was a sardonic look in it, Main fancied. He was right; Kennet was a petty officer of much experience of men and he had summed up Jimmy from the start. No real guts. The look in his eye said something like that, and it was acting as a stiffener on the First Lieutenant, who had his pride.

Just then Able Seaman Gizzard started humming. Main knew the tune: a hoary one, all about various warrant officers' wives such as the gunner's wife and the bosun's wife who kept all manner of naval gear and personnel in curious and obviously over-large places in their anatomies. A revolting

42

ditty, though not out of place round the wardroom piano in port.

Main said, 'Pack it in, Gizzard.'

Gizzard stopped. 'Sorry, sir. Just trying to cheer us all up like, sir. Try another tune, sir, shall I?'

'No, Gizzard.'

'But – '

Something snapped in Main's head. 'Don't you damn-well argue with me, Able Seaman Gizzard, or you'll be on the bridge before the officer of the watch.'

'Yessir! Sorry, sir.' Gizzard's voice was all humble innocence. 'In this, sir? Never get there I wouldn't.'

Main began to shake. Petty Officer Kennet said warningly, 'Watch it, Gizzard, just watch it.'

Gizzard didn't say anything further but noted the way Jimmy's chest was rising and falling under the white tropical shirt. And Jimmy's eyes looked sort of mad, red and hot and blazing. Jimmy wasn't far off being in a flat spin, and a fine time to choose for it. Better not provoke him by opening his mouth again. Gizzard recognized that he had a big yap at times. Edging away from Mr Hanson's bile, Gizzard hoped Jimmy wouldn't be too long getting them all out from the tiller flat. And he thanked God for the presence of Petty Officer Kennet.

4

SOUTH AND EAST of the position where the *Caithness* lay held in the hurricane's grip a convoy was moving north from Malaya towards Rangoon on the Gulf of Martaban and was now some three hundred miles clear of the Strait of Malacca. This convoy consisted of five merchant vessels taking men, stores and equipment to the Imperial Japanese forces fighting the British in Burma. There was, of course, a land route to the north; but to use this was a painful process of pushing through thick, lush jungle with all its attendant dangers and hardships. To use it, so long as the Japanese Navy controlled the waters north from Singapore into the Bay of Bengal, would be pointless.

The convoy was attended by four escort vessels, an adequate force to beat off any attack from the British fleet, which largely and very sensibly kept principally to the western part of the Bay of Bengal, close to its base at Trincomalee. This convoy was but one of many that kept the Japanese Army in Burma supplied with men and materials and the route was an easy one where the seamen could relax except when they were hit by bad weather, which currently they were not: the ships were steaming well to the east of the hurricane and although its presence had been noted from the meteorological reports and its course plotted, none of the officers of the escort or of the convoy itself was worried about it.

So, peacefully, they sailed a placid sea, knowing that at

home in Nippon they were being honoured for the part they were all playing in support of their Emperor and his immensely powerful armies that were strangling the life out of the British presence in the East. Of course, not all the convoys had been so quiet; Commander Akitane Kuroda, senior officer of the escort in the flotilla leader *Oita*, had seen cyphered signals indicating that the convoy which had passed to the north immediately before his own had been scattered by the hurricane he had noted on the weather chart and some of the merchant ships were feared lost: and that convoy, as it had happened, had been a most important one to the interests of Nippon. The innumerable gods of Nippon must have been out of their minds, Commander Kuroda reflected disrespectfully, to have permitted such a thing to occur. Either that or the meteorologists had failed to heed their warnings. Commander Kuroda, like many of his countrymen, belonged to Shinto, Buddhism and Confucianism, all three at once, for in Nippon there was no mutual exclusiveness in religion; and this triple-headed religious mainstay caused him to believe that the signals from the gods themselves were much more to be relied upon than the maps and weather charts of the meteorologists. . . .

ii

Kennet said, 'I reckon it's a losing battle, sir.' There was almost a foot of water slopping about the deck of the tiller flat by this time. Main had watched it anxiously: the rise seemed inexorable. He had reported continually to the forebridge, and had kept in communication by voice-pipe or sound-powered telephone with all other manned compartments in the ship. Nowhere else was there any trouble: the collision bulkhead for'ard was perfectly intact, the messdecks and the galley flat were taking no water, the wardroom and cabin flat were all right, so were the gunner's store and the spaces within the ambit of the Supply PO. The engine-room and boilers were in good order apart from the regular racing of the

45

screws, and Mr Henty had been philosophical when speaking to the First Lieutenant.

'Usual dockyard cock-ups, that's all.' Any warship's engineer officer felt obliged to refer disparagingly to the work of the dockyards; it was expected of him. 'Last refit . . . cowboy job's an understatement, not that I didn't get it put right immediately, of course.'

'In that case,' the First Lieutenant began carefully, but was interrupted: Mr Henty wasn't going to be beaten by semantics. Mr Henty went on to say that all manner of things had started going wrong after the ship had left dockyard hands and thereafter he'd had to improvise. But he and his staff were equal to it, he said. Main had no need to worry about the engine-room. Short of bloody bad luck, Mr Henty reckoned, they'd be all right.

In the tiller flat, Petty Officer Kennet repeated his remark; Jimmy had seemed preoccupied and hadn't heard the first time. This time he did, and was prompted to ask a question.

'Think it's time to get out, Kennet?'

Kennet shrugged. 'Your decision, sir.'

'I know that. I'm just asking your opinion.'

'Fifty-fifty, sir. Could go on as it is. On the other hand, it could go sudden like. We just don't know, sir, do we?'

Main looked at him with dislike. Kennet was a small man, almost sparrow-like, with a dark-jowled face and those bright, sardonic eyes. He was just about old enough to be Main's father, and was sometimes as impatient as if he had been just that, an impatience that in Main's view bordered on impertinence coming from a PO to the First Lieutenant. But Kennet was a first-class seaman and appeared to be as liked on the lower deck as Tucker had been, and the knowledge of these two facts acted to put Main at a mental disadvantage. The result was that Main really didn't know how best to handle Kennet and he believed Kennet knew this very well. That had its own results: Main frequently became rattled and lost his temper. He did so this time. He said snappishly, 'That's not what I expect from a petty officer.'

'Sorry, sir.'

Kennet had no intention of sticking his neck out. It could get chopped; he knew Jimmy's sort only too well. Whatever he said would be twisted round afterwards and whispered into the skipper's ear. Not that Cameron would take any notice – Cameron, Kennet believed, knew his ship's company and was always fair. But it would rankle. And as it happened Kennet believed they were all right in the tiller flat, at least for a fair while yet, and it wasn't justifiable to abandon a vital communications centre for damage-control purposes. Currently things were as they should be: the Captain for'ard, First Lieutenant in charge aft. It was true in Kennet's opinion about a losing battle, but that was as far as it went. It hadn't come to precipitancy, or funk. Kennet was muttering about funk when something happened: once again, with extra-ordinary suddenness, there came relative quiet. No wind, and the destroyer had to some extent steadied.

'What's happened, eh?' Gizzard asked, eating chocolate again, his favourite pastime.

Kennet said, 'Eye of the storm, Stripey. We're in the dead centre.'

iii

It was a worse-than-ever feeling of doom, something really uncanny. The winds revolved about them but were heard only as a distantly eerie sound, and in their immediate vicinity the surface was oily, with a very heavy swell running. 'How long will this go on, Pilot?' Cameron asked.

'Not long,' Dawnay answered. 'The cyclonic action . . . the storm's moving pretty fast, I'd say nearly thirty knots north-west. The centre will move with it.'

'Suppose we move with it, too?'

'Stay in the eye, d'you mean?'

'Yes. Can we? What would happen, if we did?'

Dawnay said, 'Well, we'd stay in comparative calm – but the heaviest winds are immediately surrounding it, of course.

47

They'll weave across the perimeter. . . . I doubt if we could hold our position indefinitely. We'd slip back in. The centre doesn't maintain a wholly cohesive circumference.' He passed a hand across his face. 'Are you thinking of trying it?'

Cameron grinned. 'You sound reluctant, Pilot!'

'Call it fear of the unknown,' Dawnay said with an uneasy laugh. 'I've never been in the actual eye of a hurricane before!'

'Cultivate the pioneering spirit, Pilot.' Cameron lifted his glasses and studied the horizons all round. They were close and threatening as the destroyer rose and fell beneath him, climbing the shifting watery hillsides of the swell, then sliding down the other side. In the wheelhouse Shiner White was once again at the wheel, relieving the coxswain. He was sweating profusely in the close, clammy atmosphere and in spite of their unpropitious circumstances and his chief attention being on the job in hand, lewd thoughts kept on flitting through his mind. There was a thirty-five-year-old widow back in Pompey who was responsible for them: her nude body kept intruding. Big tits, big bum, lovely. She was all for it, couldn't get enough, ever. Her husband had been a chief gunner's mate, sunk aboard a battlewagon, and any matlow knew a chief gunner's mate did it by numbers and his widow was the living proof of that, reacting as if to orders, one, two, three . . . and if you were too slow to get the projy into the breech she let you know it. Shiner White, as he steered the *Caithness* to God alone knew what, felt his own reactions and knew it was a pretty bad time to have them since he saw that wet little OD, Flatt, looking and grinning. . . . He forced his thoughts to something else, something innocuous like trying to get pissed in the canteen up in Scapa on the allowance of two perishing pints of Brickwood's, but not surprisingly it didn't work and he tried to hide himself behind the support of the steering compass but kept on seeing Elsie lying on the bed just off Arundel Street in Pompey and trying not to think there was some other rotten matlow in it with her.

48

Since abstention was unlikely he had no success in that direction either.

No orders from the bridge; Shiner White held his course, following the gyro repeater and moving the wheel a little to port or a little to starboard to keep the pointer in the right position. His mind had shifted from Elsie at last and was flitting about his own old woman, a different kettle of fish, no tits to speak of and a flat bum, and not all that keen – her dad had been the sexton of a country church and on account of his position her mum had castigated such things as dirty, not the sort of thing the sexton would approve of notwithstanding that he had seven kids of his own and how *that* had come about had apparently never been specifically accounted for by Shiner White's mother-in-law. Anyway, her attitude had permeated her daughter's bedtime thinking and that was that. Very reluctant, she was. . . .

Shiner White's reverie was interrupted very suddenly. There was a high whine of wind, a whine that rose to a shriek and the navigator's voice came down the pipe: 'Cox'n on the wheel!'

'Cox'n on the wheel, sir!' Chapman, expectant of the order as violent movement of the destroyer accompanied the wind, was already shouldering White aside. There were no orders as to any alteration of course or speed; but once again Dawnay's voice came down, this time informatively.

'We're back in it, Cox'n.'

'Aye, sir. Didn't last long, sir.'

No response. On the open bridge spray was flying across and spume covered the water, making it look like a solid carpet of foam. A vast wave loomed through it, breaking the pattern right ahead as it raced towards the plunging destroyer and then dropped slap on to the fo'c'sle head, twisting the barrel of Number One gun until it was pointed up-and-down, aimed for the plating over the seamen's messdeck, with the gun-shield virtually flattened behind it. The bows went down, down . . . just as though the ship were in a dive from which she wasn't going to come up again. Sea rose over both for'ard guns, rose almost to the level of the fore screen of the bridge. The yeoman of the watch, holding fast with his hands to his flag locker, dangled with his feet in the air like a puppet on a string. Midshipman Tillotson, something of a spare hand now that Dawnay had taken over the watch, shot forward and crashed full tilt into Cameron, who was forced hard against the metal and glass of the fore screen.

There was no breath in Tillotson even to apologize. Cameron glanced at his face. The snotty, he saw, was dead scared, no doubt convinced the end was not far off.

'It's all right, Mid,' he said. 'We're seaworthy yet.'

'Yessir,' Tillotson said on a heaving breath, then asked, 'Have you seen weather as bad as this, sir?'

'There's always a first time,' Cameron answered. 'But we're not unique, you know. Men have sailed these waters for a hell of a long time, and come through.' He was having to shout into the midshipman's ear: the racket was worse than ever and to take breath against the wind's fury was almost impossible now. Inside himself Cameron wondered that they were holding together at all; every rivet in the ship, above the waterline and below, would be taking an immense strain. Engineers could moan about dockyards and dockyard mateys and lousy refits until they were blue in the face, but the old *Caithness* was Devonport built and she was good and sound, she had to be if she could take this without giving up the ghost. The West Country dockyard mateys could be proud of their workmanship.

But it was no more than seconds later that trouble came.

iv

Below in the tiller flat they didn't, in the end, have much time. When the ship's head went down at its steep angle, the stern was lifted high in the air, like a duck seeking fish beneath its body. The screws, racing as they had done so many times before, sent shudders through the whole of the after part; and there was a curious and alarming waggle, again like the fish-seeking duck, this time shaking out its tail feathers. Petty Officer Kennet shouted a warning as he saw the sprung plates widen and admit a streak of daylight. Then the ship began to straighten out, the stern falling back so that the sea took the screws once again in its grip and the steering engine started its chatter as the coxswain in the wheelhouse kept the ship on her course. Then, as the plates submerged aft, the water came in, spurting with tremendous force across the enclosed space of the tiller flat, taking Sub-Lieutenant Hanson in the small of the back and knocking him to the deck.

'Out, sir, and batten down!' Kennet yelled at the First Lieutenant, then saw that he didn't need to: Jimmy was already on his way, reaching up for the hatch and heaving himself through. He stayed on the outside, looking down as the rest of the hands followed his motion. Kennet made a guess at what Jimmy would say afterwards: he'd got out first so as to supervise the evacuation and stand by to clip down the hatch against the rising water. After Main, the first man through was Ordinary Seaman Burden, propelled on his way by Petty Officer Kennet who always had a thought for the youngsters, no more than kids really, and after him the ERA, Walsh.

Then Stripey Gizzard, gut and all, in such a hurry that he cracked his head on the coaming, a real whopper that stunned him. He hung there, dazed and uncertain, filling the entire space. From below Hanson and Kennet pushed and shoved and cursed; from above the First Lieutenant and Burden pulled. By now the water was up to Kennet's shoulders and he was in fact afloat, with not much shove behind him. Likewise Hanson. Something drastic had happened to Able Seaman Gizzard: one leg seemed to be through the hatch; the other was wedged below so that his crutch had impacted against the coaming and he had become immovable. Kennet, as the water rose to his chin, wondered desperately how the bloody hell Gizzard had achieved the almost impossible.

The water rose around Gizzard's body, seeping through the hatch at first and then, as the pressure mounted, zipping through forcefully and coming in heavy jets to start flooding the compartment above the tiller flat. Main moved for'ard to call the bridge by the sound-powered telephone on the wardroom bulkhead. He was intercepted by the Surgeon Lieutenant.

'The Jap, Number One. He's round.'

Main said, 'Oh, bugger the Jap.' Getting the bridge, he reported the tiller flat flooded and Able Seaman Gizzard jammed in the hatch, which couldn't be clipped down. He wanted more hands sent aft soonest possible. Dawnay said that would be seen to; and Ordinary Seaman Flatt was sent down, dangerously, to the galley flat to pass the word to Leading Seaman Prosser, who had taken over in place of Petty Officer Tucker lost overboard. Prosser, reaching the scene, found that the only practicable way of removing Gizzard was by way of pulley-hauley; and a tackle was set up, with difficulty as the water surged through the hatch. Gizzard was glad enough of rescue but yelled with the agonizing pain and passed out cold when the rope of the tackle was passed around his chest and he was hoisted clear by sweating seamen tailing on to the purchase. Once he was free, Main ordered the hatch cover to be shut and the clips slammed on hard and fast. Easier said than done: it took all hands and a lot of force to get the cover down against the upflow of the water from below, but they did it. When the hatch was closed Main passed a hand over his face and staggered back against the bulkhead behind him. He was shaking like a leaf and his legs felt weak, as though they wouldn't take his weight much longer. Styles, who had come along to help where he could, looked at him in concern but Main muttered that he was all right. He had to report in person to the bridge: anything to get out into the open air now.

He made his way for'ard along the lifeline and reached the ladder leading to the bridge, where he hung for a moment, feeling faint. The ship was wallowing as though out of control, being flung this way and that by the action of the waves, as though she were dead. Then he realized: the rising water had submerged the steering engine, and it had stopped, and the ship was unable to steer by main steering. Or, with the tiller flat totally flooded, by emergency steering either. There was in fact the secondary steering position aft of the searchlight platform but this was out of action, one of Henty's moans about the dockyard. The whole show was jammed up solid, Henty had reported, and all his engine-room staff, like all the king's horses, couldn't put it to together again.

Main heaved himself up the ladder and made his report to the Captain. Cameron took it in silence: Sub-Lieutenant Hanson and Petty Officer Kennet, submerged in the tiller flat. Dead by now, obviously. Cameron wouldn't comment, wouldn't lay blame, until he had a chance to find out the facts. Main appeared to be a sick man: conscience at work already? So far it was impossible to judge his First Lieutenant's actions. His duty as damage-control officer had been clear enough and in fact he had done it: he had got the hatch shut as soon as possible, as soon as Gizzard had been extricated. And he could not have risked the delay involved in going down to look for men who were probably already dead by that time. In any case, the upward pressure of water would have made descent impossible. But Cameron would be finding out why Main had got out himself with men left below. And, as his command wallowed at the ocean's will, he was left with the reflection that Hanson and Kennet had in fact died because Able Seaman Gizzard had been unable to control his appetite. Lost by stomach action.

5

'ONLY ONE THING for it, Pilot. Steer by main engines. Or try to.'

Easier said than done, Dawnay thought, but knew it was the only possible thing that could be attempted. Below in the engine-room Henty swore luridly each time the telegraph rang from the wheelhouse under orders from the bridge: half ahead starboard, stop port, half astern port . . . and then the other way around as Cameron tried to bring the ship's head over to starboard, and then again, and again, and again, an engineer officer's nightmare of spinning shafts going this way and that and still, every now and again, racing dangerously. But of course the skipper had to keep the head pointing into wind and sea. That was vital. Once come broadside to those bloody great waves, Henty thought, and they'd had it, no hope. And he thanked God that despite the worst efforts of the last dockyard they'd visited, his engines were bearing up. They were going to be the ship's salvation, no doubt about that.

The word had spread along the messdecks – seamen, stokers, communications and miscellaneous – as to what Stripey Gizzard had achieved: two men dead, an officer and a PO. All because old Stripey had got stuck fast like an eggbound hen. Of course, the way he'd cracked his skull hadn't helped. You had to laugh about something at sea in wartime; if you didn't, you'd go clean round the bend. No one

54

actually laughed about losing two of the ship's company but there was the funny side and it resulted in some coarse jokes.

'That's right,' Leading Seaman Prosser said sardonically. 'Get it out of the system and then shut your gobs. I don't want to hear any more about it once Stripey's back in circulation.'

That, they understood: Stripey would be bound to have it on his conscience. Word had come through from aft that he was to be under observation for twenty-four hours, by which time, presumably, the quack would know for sure if he'd suffered brain damage. The general opinion along the messdecks was that Stripey Gizzard's head was too thick and solid for that, it was like the armoured belt of the *King George V*. Possibly not so the First Lieutenant: the messdecks were buzzing with much more than what Stripey had done by sheer accident. It hadn't been any accident, the buzz said, that had propelled Jimmy the One up through the tiller-flat hatch before anyone else. And he didn't look as thick as Stripey; he was more the nervy sort. He often had a kind of haunted look about him, as though he wasn't happy in the service, as though everything was a bit much for him. He could go to pieces now. It was obvious the skipper couldn't turn a blind eye; and Jimmy RN wasn't going to like being bollocked good and proper by the RNVR.

ii

The problem was very much on Cameron's mind as he conned the *Caithness* through the howl and batter of the storm, watching the ship's head constantly, eyes red and sore from the salt and the sting of the wind, his whole body aching with the never-ending effort of simply fighting the ship's violent movement with his body, bracing himself one way and then the other. Time meant nothing now: they had been in the hurricane's grip for some thirty-six hours but it might have been centuries. It was as though a time without storm had never existed; it was becoming a way of life. It was the same with Dawnay: one or two reliefs had in fact been made despite

55

the weather – the signalmen, the bridge messenger, the telegraphsman in the wheelhouse had all been relieved. But some could not be and had to remain at their stations until they came through the storm. Cameron, of course, was one; Dawnay another. And it was the same for CPO Chapman and Leading Seaman White, and Mr Henty. After a while you acquired a second wind as it were; and there was the Surgeon Lieutenant's medical assistance – he made the rounds of the ship himself, not wanting to expose his SBA to the dangers of the upper deck, handing out benzedrine tablets to the watchkeepers.

'This'll keep you going,' he said. 'You'll be on edge after the effect wears off, but for now you'll feel fine.'

'Never took drugs before, sir,' the coxswain said looking at the pill in his palm doubtfully.

'Don't look on it as a drug, Cox'n. I promise you, you won't become addicted. Just a one-off thing.'

'If you say so, sir.' Chapman swallowed, felt no effect whatsoever and said so.

Styles laughed. 'Patience, Cox'n. Give it time.'

'As the woman,' Shiner White put in, 'said to the bloke who couldn't get it up – '

'That's enough of that, Leading Seaman White,' Chapman said.

Styles laughed again. 'Oh, don't mind me. I know the facts of life.' He went on his way, out into the tearing wind, holding tight to anything that offered a hand-hold, climbing the swaying ladder to the bridge where he doled out his pills to Cameron and the navigator, who took them without query. Styles lifted an eye at the officer of the watch, now another of the RNVR lieutenants, Alan Ringrose, who'd had some recent sleep. 'You? Or not? I only like to issue them when absolutely necessary.'

Ringrose shook his head. 'No, thanks, Doc. Not being indispensable, I'll probably get a relief some time. How's Gizzard?'

Styles shrugged. 'He'll pull through.'

'More than he did in the – '

'Yes.' Styles' voice was flat but firm. He knew the strains on Cameron and he deplored any levity about what had happened, not that Cameron would be likely to overhear in the wind's racket; and he was worried, too, about Number One. Main needed the opposite of benzedrine: he needed a sedative but was currently occupied about the ship, making sure that there was no further damage anywhere, and he couldn't be spared from his duty. As soon as the ship was through, Styles would have a word with him. With the Captain, if necessary. He wanted to have a word about his prisoner patient, too – the Japanese seaman. Before leaving the bridge he reported to Cameron as he had already reported to Number One – that the man was comfortable, or as comfortable as he could possibly be with his broken limbs and the ship's movement, and could be questioned.

Cameron nodded. 'Thank you, Doctor. First things first, though.'

'Yes, sir. Anything I can do? Ask the questions?'

Cameron said, 'Well, that's a point, I suppose. As a matter of fact it might come better from you. But is it ethical? I mean, in accordance with your Hippocratic oath, and the Geneva thing?'

'I've really no idea. Have you?'

'No. That makes two of us. Bloody ignoramuses . . . we'll take a chance, Doc. I want to know anything that might be useful – make a note of anything he comes out with. In particular, Japanese naval movements, the name and details of his own ship – you know the sort of thing, it's all common sense really.' Cameron paused. 'God knows why I've only just thought of this, but what about the language problem? I don't speak Japanese! Do you?'

'No, I don't,' Styles said, 'but not to worry. He has enough English. Pidgin, but understandable.'

'When he wants to, I suspect,' Cameron said drily. 'Just do your best, Doc.' He had an urge to ask the Surgeon Lieutenant if he knew what had gone on in the tiller flat, but he refrained. It wasn't the Doc's job; not yet, anyway. He had to find things out for himself and then make some decisions. In the meantime he knew the feeling in the ship wouldn't be good. With two corpses trapped in the flooded tiller flat – and there was no prospect of being able to pump out until they could effect a makeshift repair from outboard of the sprung plates – there would be plenty of men capable of seeing ghosts or anyway seeing all kinds of doom aboard a floating coffin unable to steer. Those corpses would be on every man's mind as the *Caithness* strained and fought and wallowed and her engines constantly changed their speed and thrust. And they would all know about Number One. The mood would be fractious to say the least. There were one or two sea lawyers loose on the lower deck and they would almost certainly be stirring up a witch's brew of comment, prophecy and insubordination.

iii

'Not understand,' the Japanese said, black eyes staring up at Styles.

'No? What's your name?'

'Not understand.'

'Really.' The Doctor, sitting beside the Japanese in the sick-bay cot to which he had been transferred when it had been vacated, kept his tone pleasant and easy. 'Like a drink of water, would you?'

'Yes please, thank you.'

'Understood that all right.' Styles gestured at the SBA, who brought a glass of water. The Japanese drank. 'Now you're lubricated, how about understanding a little more?'

'Not understand.'

'What's your name? You'll have to tell us that, if you want your relations in Japan to know you've been picked up and are safe as a prisoner of war.'

It was quite a long speech; the man appeared to understand it well enough. He said, 'Hiroshi Kondo.'

'And you're a seaman.'

'Not understand.'

'Oh, for Buddha's sake! How stupid can you get! Of course you understand, and anyway it's obvious enough you're a seaman, isn't it?'

The Japanese grinned, black eyes wide and glittering. 'Of course, yes. But will not assist dirty pigs of English. Will say nothing. Not have to, under terms of Geneva Convention.'

Styles leaned forward, his face hardening. 'Don't forget where you are, Hiroshi Kondo. Don't forget I'm the doctor. I can make life pretty hard for you if I so choose, you know.'

'Yes. But you will not. Nasty treatment, sadism, will be reported in due course to British General Medical Council. In Nippon, when not at war, am not seaman. Am lawyer's clerk.'

Styles gave a short, hard laugh and got to his feet. He was stymied, not a chance of getting any answers; and of course there would be no harsh treatment, that went without saying; he was a medical man before anything else, war or no war. However, just as he left the sick bay, a sudden thought came to Styles and he beckoned the SBA out into the alleyway. 'The little bugger's gear,' he said. 'What was done with it?'

'Bundled up when I stripped him off, sir.'

'Did you examine it?'

'No, sir. Never thought about it. Soaked and dirty – '

'Yes, no doubt. Where is it now?'

'Shoved it in the wardroom pantry, sir – '

'Oh, very hygienic!'

'In a rush, sir, to get the Jap seen to.'

'All right, Griffin. I'm going to check it over, you never know. There could be clues.' Styles went through to the pantry: Able Seaman Urridge, wardroom messman, was wedged in a corner as comfortably as possible, reading a paperback with a nude woman on the cover. He pushed it out of sight when he saw the doctor. Doctors were weird, and might make diagnoses, right or wrong, when they encountered a reservist of middle years reading about nude young women.

Styles said, 'All right, Urridge, I've seen it already. I take it you're not busy?'

'Not really busy like, sir, no – '

'Then I'd like you to produce the bundle of clothing that my SBA chucked in here.'

'Yessir.' Urridge got to his feet and lurched over to another corner of the pantry. He picked up the still sodden bundle and held it at arm's length, his nose wrinkled up. 'Here it is, sir. It wouldn't have been, if I'd been able to get on deck and chuck it over with the gash. Gash is still here an' all.' Styles could smell it: two days' accumulation of plate scrapings and general dustbin muck. Ships battened down at sea were never fresh-smelling and in hurricanes they suffered more, became mobile tips.

'Spread it out, Urridge,' Styles said.

'Sure it's healthy, sir?' Urridge looked very doubtful, as though he might already have caught the plague.

'Salt water is a useful antiseptic, Urridge.'

'Speaking as a doctor, sir?'

'Speaking as a doctor. But if you're so worried I'll do it myself.' Styles had an idea that had Urridge not been concerned about strange Oriental diseases he would already have been through the clothing if only to seek souvenirs. 'Drop it on the deck, Urridge.'

Thankfully, Urridge did so. Doctors, he'd always heard, were immune. It was up to them to use their immunity to do the dirty work themselves. He went back to his corner, keeping well clear as if he expected a swarm of angry germs to have survived the sea just so they could buzz straight at him the moment they were disturbed. From his corner he couldn't see the doc's busy hands and didn't particularly want to, rooting about in a bundle of old clothes, motley stuff that didn't look very much like uniform. Could mean the Jap was from a merchant ship, but it didn't have to. In the British Navy, at any rate in cold climates, they all wore all manner of weird gear at sea and probably the little yellow buggers did too. Them and their bloody emperor . . . Hirohito, Musso and Adolf, they were all the same and Able Seaman Urridge loathed the lot of them and loathed General Franco too. Urridge was a socialist, the natural enemy of all of them, though he kept his politics to himself since he liked his soft number as wardroom messman even though he classed officers along with Hirohito, Musso, Adolf and Franco. It was nice to be able to sneer at them inwardly while calling them sir. One day, soon as the war was won, things would change. And he wouldn't have to sit within range of dirty Jap germs while the Doc rootled about like a pig in a sty. All he would find would be the germs.

But it wasn't: Styles didn't let on to Urridge what he'd found but Urridge knew he'd found something that had excited him. Having found it, he told Urridge to restow the junk and then, according to what Urridge reported in the messdeck later on, buggered off out of the pantry, fast.

iv

Styles made his way to the bridge. He fancied that at long last a little of the weight had gone out of the wind though the seas were mountainous still, crossing a very heavy swell. On the bridge Cameron also had noted a lessening of the wind. According to Dawnay that could mean they were coming clear, that they had passed, or rather had been passed by, the storm and they had in fact been left behind by the fringe. Just before the wind had lessened it had been more appalling than before, and this, Dawnay said, was a characteristic of the fringe, the outer edge. He had prophesied that they would quite suddenly leave the wind behind them.

Just as the Surgeon Lieutenant reached the bridge, they did. It was extraordinary. The wind fell right away and they could see the storm ahead, moving away from them towards the horizon. It would be a long while yet, however, before they met calm water.

As Cameron turned with an expression of sheer relief, Styles saluted.

'Yes, Doc, what is it?'

'The prisoner, sir.'

'Oh – yes.' It was as though Cameron had forgotten all about the matter. 'Any luck?'

'Not with the man himself. Full non-cooperation there.'

'I thought there might be. But?'

Styles grinned. 'Yes, sir – but. His clothing. I found two things of interest. A stencil on his oilskin: *Tamara Maru*. I take it to be a ship name – '

'Right, it would be. And the *Maru* indicates a merchant ship. Might just as well have told you, mightn't he? What else, Doc?'

'This,' Styles said, and held something out to Cameron. Cameron took it wonderingly: it was a British soldier's pay book. Tucked into the sodden mess was an equally sodden five-pound note. The slim book was made out in the name of Gorman, Peter Charles, sergeant, Royal Artillery.

Cameron said, 'That could tell a story, couldn't it?'

'I think it's already told one,' Styles said. 'Just look at the last official entry. See where it was made, and the date?'

Cameron nodded. It was still readable. 'Singapore, 10 February 1942.'

'Just before the surrender, sir.'

'So Sergeant Gorman became a prisoner of the Japs?'

'That's what appears to be the case, yes.'

'I wonder how he hung on to the pay book, for God's sake!'

Styles shrugged. 'The ingenuity of the British soldier. He managed it – until Hiroshi Kondo got his hands on it. The question now is, where and when did Hiroshi Kondo get it?'

'Yes. Maybe we can use this to put pressure on him.'

Styles said, 'I doubt if it would engender much pressure. We're not going to charge him with theft, are we? Wouldn't be much skin off his little Jap nose if we did, come to that.' He paused. He could see that Cameron was all in, scarcely able to think straight. He went on, 'I think it's telling us more of the story as it is, sir. We can take it that Kondo, as a seaman, wouldn't have been likely to have been around the POW camps. They're a military responsibility – and in any case Kondo seems to have been a merchant seaman of sorts, possibly a steward, or a purser's assistant very likely – '

'Why a purser's assistant?'

'He told me he was a lawyer's clerk in peacetime. The two things could slot in. If I'm right, he's come from a liner, and most probably – in fact certainly – one that's being used as a transport.'

'Troop transport?'

Styles nodded. 'Something going between Rangoon and Malaya, let's say.'

'So he picked up this pay book aboard a transport?'

'I think so, yes.'

'With British troops aboard. . . .'

'Sergeant Gorman, anyway.'

'Scarcely on his own,' Cameron said. He was reeling from near exhaustion; he reached out to the binnacle for support. Styles said it was time he turned in for a spell and let the First Lieutenant have the ship. Dawnay too was as tired as Cameron and also needed to get below as soon as it was possible. Cameron brushed the doctor metaphorically aside. He couldn't, he said, leave the bridge yet, not with the tiller flat flooded and the ship unable to steer other than by engines. In any case, Main would have his hands full seeing to a running repair and then the pumping out of the tiller flat. Cameron went back to the question of the pay book and the queries it raised. He said, 'British troops on the move. What do you think, Pilot?'

Dawnay shrugged. 'Doesn't have to be that, sir. That Jap could have come by it in a dozen different ways. It's all guesswork on the Doc's part.'

'But if the doctor's right? He could be . . . and I've a hunch he is. And that means the *Tamara Maru* was northbound. There are plenty of our chaps shut up in Malaya but there wouldn't be any British troops to bring south from any ports in Burma – '

'The Japs'll have taken prisoners,' Dawnay interrupted.

'They could be sending them south to Malaya, or even all the way to Japan.'

'I don't think so,' Cameron said. 'Last time we were in Trinco, I got some intelligence from the staff – classified, of course, but now's the time to talk about it.' He paused, rubbing at his eyes, and wedged himself upright against the roll and pitch, a nasty corkscrew motion. 'The Japs weren't sending any prisoners out of Burma, apparently. They're using them as forced labour, building bridges and railways and so on, and clearing jungle sites for the Jap operations. It's possible they haven't got enough prisoners for their needs.'

'You mean – '

'I mean this,' Cameron said. 'They could be sending our troops up north, from the POW camps in Malaya, to live out a hell in the Burmese jungle. If that's the case, then there could be more convoys coming through – and we happen to be not so far off the convoy route from Rangoon. It's up to us to do something about it.'

Dawnay blew out a long breath. 'Perhaps. But what, exactly?'

'I don't know yet. Intercept.'

'And sink?'

'If we have to, yes.'

'And pick up a troopship-ful of brown jobs? Where's the room for that, sir?'

'We'd cope if we had to. But there could be other ways . . . if we can deal with the escort, we could bring the transports in under our guns. The convoys won't be heavily escorted in these waters, Pilot. The Japs have it all their own way.' He added with a grin, 'Except for us, that is.'

'On our own?'

'It'll have to be. I can't break wireless silence to make a report to Trinco – the moment I do that the game's up. If they know a British warship's in the vicinity, either they'll strengthen their escorts or they'll hold the convoys back. We'll take a look at the chart, Pilot.'

As the weather eased, so the conditions eased below decks. Battened-down doors and hatches were opened up and fresh air blew through the ship. Mr Henty came up at last from the starting platform and with Chief ERA Trigg went over the side on a bosun's chair, dangerously as there was still a swell running, to take a close look at the sprung plates. He reported to the Captain that once the swell had gone down sufficiently he would be able to make a repair that would last so long as they didn't meet more bad weather; but he added a warning that a lengthy period at sea wouldn't do the repair much good.

'Just do your best, Chief,' Cameron said. 'There may be some British troops in the vicinity who'll be bloody glad to see us if you can keep us afloat.'

'She'll float all right,' Henty said with a sniff. 'I did hear a buzz, sir, about Jap transports with – '

'Three cheers for the galley wireless,' Cameron said. He told Henty what he intended to do. Henty shook his head lugubriously but offered no comment. He was just the engineer, the bloke that was going to get the ship out of a hole. If he could. Later that day the swell went down enough and he did. With Trigg and two more engine-room artificers, and some seamen to assist with the pulley-hauley work, and the First Lieutenant leaning over the guardrail aft fooling himself that he was in overall charge, Mr Henty as it were plugged the gap and made all shipshape. After that, they pumped out the flooded compartment so that the steering engine could be dried out, checked, greased and put in running order again. As the water level dropped, the bodies could be seen, bumping about the plates and pipes and steering gear, Hanson and Kennet, bloated and flaccid, a sadly gruesome sight. Main reported to the bridge.

'The bodies, sir.'

'Get them up, Number One.' Cameron's tone was flat, expressionless. Main, largely responsible for their deaths, was not meeting his eye. 'See to it that they're sewn up right away.'

'Aye, aye, sir. You'll take the committal?'

'The moment you're ready, yes.'

Main saluted and turned away down the starboard ladder. Cameron watched him making his way aft. He didn't envy him: the whole ship must know the facts. Of course, to a large extent it had been sheer foul luck: Gizzard's gut. And you couldn't put a stomach in the rattle, bring it before the officer of the watch on a charge of obstruction. Gizzard would be feeling very bad about it too. But it came down to Main; he'd been the officer in charge. There would have to be words about that soon. Main would be given his chance to offer an explanation before Cameron came to any decisions, even in his mind. As a captain, you had to keep your mind open until such time as it was closed by the presentation of hard facts. Hanson and Kennet would have had a lot to offer in regard to fact if they hadn't been dead. Now they were about to be sewn up in the usual canvas shrouds, Kennet in his own hammock, Hanson in a spare provided by the buffer, Petty Officer Bustacle. Lead weights at the feet, to ensure sinking. And himself reading the short, simple service, and standing at the salute as the bodies slid down the tilted plank from beneath the folds of the White Ensign.

It was well into the night, and the committal service was in the past, when the warrant engineer came to the bridge. In the interval both Cameron and Dawnay had managed to snatch a couple of hours' sleep apiece, and had bathed and shifted into clean clothing. Cameron was, as Styles had prophesied, on edge from the after effects of the benzedrine. But he didn't let it show when Mr Henty appeared.

Henty reported, 'Steering engine ready for testing, sir.'

'Well done indeed, Chief – and thank you.'

Henty gave a grunt. 'We'll see if the bugger works first, sir.' Cameron passed a helm order to the Coxswain in the wheelhouse. The wheel went over: there was a highly satisfactory sound from the telemotor steering gear. All was well according to the Coxswain.

Cameron passed down, 'Starboard ten.'

'Starboard ten, sir. Ten of starboard wheel on, sir.'

Cameron watched the swing of the ship's head across the dark water, the jackstaff in the bows moving across a sky that was beginning to light with stars. Already he had worked things out with the navigating officer. He steadied the ship on 090 degrees and then spoke personally to Chief PO Chapman.

'Right, Cox'n. Fall yourself out – we'll revert to the ordinary quartermaster watches for now.'

'Aye, aye, sir.' The relief in Chapman's voice was very plain.

Cameron moved across to the microphone of the Tannoy. He picked it up, switched on. His voice went to all parts of the destroyer where men were on watch or at last turning in for a few hours' sleep. 'This is the Captain speaking. You'll all have heard buzzes; here are the facts.' He paused. '*Caithness* is proceeding towards the Burma coast in order to cross the Japanese convoy route from Malaya to Rangoon. I suspect British prisoners of war are being transported north to become forced labour for the Japs. I propose to intercept the next convoy. As soon as I pick up that convoy, and at this moment I have no knowledge of its whereabouts, the ship will go to action stations. That is all.'

6

THE HURRICANE had swept the destroyer along with it, the sheer weight of wind and the force of the sea overcoming the course being steered at any one time. So there was a lot of water to cover before they could in fact say they were lying across the convoy track.

Pegram, taking the forenoon watch on the bridge next day – for the time being the ship had reverted to the normal three-watch system of four hours on and eight off – turned as he heard the voice behind him.

'Lieutenant Pegram, sir.' It was Petty Officer Jago, gunner's mate, usually known as the gunnery instructor.

'Yes, GI?'

'Guns, sir,' Jago said briefly. 'Gun drill.'

Pegram, in addition to his watchkeeping and divisional duties, was the gunnery officer. 'What about it?'

'Could be in action soon, sir.'

'You mean you want to exercise action.' Pegram stifled a sigh: he'd been landed with the job of gunnery officer but guns failed to inspire much devotion in him, though as a conscientious officer he did his best, and he knew it was considered not a bad best. All the same, be believed Petty Officer Jago suspected his basic lack of commitment – Jago lived and breathed guns himself and always moved about the decks as though he were gaitered and pipeclayed ready for the Commodore's Guard at RNB or to take over as gunner's mate of the parade at Whale Island, the Portsmouth gunnery school which Jago regarded as his personal paradise.

Jago responded to Pegram's statement. 'Yes, sir. Get slack, they do, if they're not chivvied up.'

Pegram grinned. 'The guns?'

'Not the guns, sir.' Jago's face was stiff. He disliked flippancy from gunnery officers. 'Guns' crews, sir.'

'Yes, quite. All right, GI. I'll speak to the First Lieutenant.'

'Thank you, sir.' Jago remained where he was, beside Pegram, rigid at attention, not an easy job in a ship that was still rolling to a slight swell left behind, even now, by the hurricane. Pegram responded as evidently required.

He said formally, 'Carry on, please, Petty Officer Jago.'

'Sir!' Jago gave a smart salute and turned about. He marched away, breaking step to descend the ladder. He reached the fo'c'sle, an act of masochism: that there Number One gun, what a sight! Jago's heart bled for twisted metal that he was convinced could feel its degradation. And nothing to be done about it till they got back to Trinco, and maybe not even there. Trincomalee dockyard, they had the cheek to call it . . . they'd never cope with a bashed-up gun-barrel, not they! One gun gone, three left – three 4.7-inch plus the ack-ack and the close-range weapons. Should be enough to deal with the sort of escort the Japs were said to provide for their convoys, but sod-all use against anything bigger than a destroyer. If their luck was out and the Japs sent in a cruiser . . . but never say die, Petty Officer Jago said to himself, even if the skipper was barmy enough to attack a convoy single-handed and with a quarter of his main armament gone for a burton. Jago thought he was barmy, but would never have said so. Loyalty was important, and you had to keep the discipline going in a ship crammed with hostilities-only ratings, ordinary seamen from God knew what occupations, all far removed from the sea. Farm hands, teachers, auction-eers' assistants, counter jumpers, bus conductors to name a few.

Number Two gun alone had four erstwhile landlubbers in

69

its crew. Jago spoke to one of them. 'You. Ordinary Seaman Burden.'

'Me, GI?'

'Just said so, didn't I? Learned any more about guns, have you?'

'I think so, GI.'

'Think so! Ought to bloody *know* so, lad! No time for thinking, not at sea. Swing back the britch – sharp.'

Burden obeyed, moving the lever and opening up the breech. Jago put a finger on a piece of the mechanism. 'What's that called, eh?'

Burden said, 'Catch retaining breech – '

'Britch is how you pronounce it. For God's sake! You don't wear *breeches*, you wear *britches*, right?'

'I don't wear either, GI,' Burden said with a grin. 'Maybe my granddad – '

'And don't be impertinent, Ordinary Seaman Burden, or you'll be on the bridge in one-one-two. *Britch*. Now, let's have it again, proper.'

'Catch retaining britch block open, GI.'

'Right. And don't forget it.' Jago marched away, broke step again for the ladder down from the break of the fo'c'sle, and marched aft, left-right-left, arms swinging. Something had been achieved. Jago liked precision in all things: precise speech made for precise gunnery. One of Jago's pet hates was the way bleeding landlubbers always talked about *breeches* buoys . . . like the perishing BBC when they announced some inshore sea rescue on the news. Didn't bother to think: you *sat* in the bloody buoy like you were pulling on your britches, which was why it was so called. But anyone who'd never been to sea was dim witted, stood to reason.

And that Pegram. Called himself the gunnery officer! Enough to make the cat pee itself. He was a decent bloke, all right, and probably safe on the bridge or the skipper wouldn't have worn him long, but what he knew about guns wouldn't be visible on sixpence. But Jago was nevertheless philosophical: it left him in *de facto* charge of his own department.

The *Caithness* didn't carry a warrant gunner; only a gunner (T) which wasn't the same thing at all. Torpedoes, in Jago's view, didn't count. Nor did torpedo-gunners' mates, who were a sloppy lot from a sloppy depot. HMS *Vernon*, the torpedo school at Portsmouth, was a very different kettle of fish from Whaley, which was why Whaley's ship-name was HMS *Excellent*. Sloppy Joes were the torpedo party. Technicians and all-electric.

One of them was making his way for'ard as Jago proceeded aft and they met beneath the searchlight platform amidships: Mr Clinch, GUNNER(T), RN, in person.

'Morning, GI.'

'Morning, sir.' Jago saluted, eyeing Mr Clinch narrowly. White tropical shirt a shade of grey, one shoulder-strap with its single thin gold stripe hanging judas down his arm.

Mr Clinch saw Jago's pointed stare. He grinned and dug a finger into the GI's ribs, which Jago didn't go much on. Familiarity was bad for discipline. Clinch said, 'I don't need to offer you a penny for 'em, GI. Old rag-bag, that's what you're thinking, right?'

'Certainly not, sir.' Jago gazed over the warrant officer's head. 'Wouldn't think like that, sir.' Jago always made much of the 'sir' when speaking to officers but more so when speaking to warrant officers. Jago expected to be a warrant officer himself one day: Mr Jago, Gunner, RN. And then maybe he'd make the wardroom as a lieutenant. Rare, but it could be done so long as you were keen, efficient and kept your nose clean. Maybe just a little sucking-up along the way. Not too obvious, of course, but it was more sensible than making enemies of the officers under whom you were serving. Petty Officer Jago very much liked the sound of Lieutenant Jago; and he knew someone else who would like it even more: Mrs Jago. Not his wife, for Jago was a single man, dedicated to the service with no time for anything else, but his mother. His mother would bask in his reflected glory if he made it in time. He probably would. His mother was no chicken, of course, but she was a stayer. She wouldn't let the Lord take her before her son had at least made warrant rank. Then he would have achieved parity with his grandfather: Mrs Jago's dad had been a boatswain about the time of Rear-Admiral the Earl of Clanwilliam who'd commanded the Flying Squadron, under sail. Her husband, Petty Officer Jago's dad, hadn't made it at all. He'd been disrated as a petty officer, back to leading seaman, after coming back aboard pissed as a newt one night in Malta. He had never managed to climb the ladder again. It was a sore point; Jago's father, now dead, was never mentioned.

A lot of this was running through Jago's mind when Mr Clinch spoke again, making a request. Mr Clinch said, 'I was looking for you, as a matter of fact.'

'Yes, sir?'

'Got a couple of my torpedo party on light duty . . . injuries sustained in the bad weather. Spare two hands from the gunner's party, can you? I need to overhaul the tubes.'

'See what I can do, sir,' Jago said. 'When d'you want 'em, eh?'

'No time like the present.' Clinch added, 'I'll want 'em most of the afternoon as well, all right?'

Jago said he'd see to it right away, and marched off to pass the word to the leading hand of the gunner's party. Mr Clinch, he'd seemed grateful, and every little helped. Mr Clinch, when his opinion was asked by Jimmy or the skipper, would report that Petty Officer Jago was always helpful and willing. Jago was in blissful ignorance of the fact that Mr Clinch was staring after him along the deck and wondering how so much starch managed to withstand so much seawater.

ii

Earlier, Cameron, in his disturbing thoughts about the First Lieutenant, had reflected on sea lawyers. It was Able Seaman Urridge he'd had particularly in mind. Urridge, in his view, had an unpleasant face and was too obsequious to be true. His oily, ingratiating manner was patently false and hid a twisted mind that had shown itself more than once when he'd been up at Captain's Defaulters on various charges, mostly minor ones it was true. He had exhibited an amazing ability to distort facts. He advanced devious arguments in his favour and had obviously made a study of King's Regulations and Admiralty Instructions to the point where his knowledge of them exceeded that of the coxswain – who in a small ship acted as master-at-arms, head of the ship's police – and also of Cameron. And looking aft at the time that Jago had come to the bridge to speak to Pegram, Cameron had caught sight of Able Seaman Urridge, loafing on the searchlight platform and talking to an ordinary seaman named Roebuck, an HO rating also known for being exceptionally keen on what he called his rights. Urridge had been talking behind his hand after gesturing down towards the depth-charge racks aft, where the First Lieutenant had been seen proceeding a minute earlier. Roebuck was nodding in agreement and Cameron was pretty sure he knew the gist of what was being said.

It was a situation that had to be met head on. There was time to deal with it now that they were well clear of the hurricane and there must be no further delay.

'I'm going below to my cabin, Pegram,' Cameron said.

'Yes, sir.'

'Call me immediately, of course, if necessary. And send down to Number One, please. I'd like a word with him.'

'Aye, aye, sir.'

Pegram passed the message down to the wheelhouse. Cameron went down the ladder, not liking what he was going to have to do. Pegram knew very well what that was: Main was due for a rocket, and the RNVR was going to find itself at a disadvantage when bollocking the RN and never mind that Cameron had the extra half stripe. It would take a good deal of guts on the part of an officer who'd been an ordinary seaman when Lieutenant Main was emerging from his four years' training at RNC Dartmouth to join the fleet as a midshipman, one of God's elect, at any rate in their own view.

All the same, Cameron was a tough nut who'd proved himself on numerous occasions in the past.

The messenger from the wheelhouse made contact with the First Lieutenant just below the searchlight platform. 'First Lieutenant, sir – '

'Yes?'

'Captain's compliments, sir. He'd like to see you in his cabin, sir.'

'All right,' Main said off-handedly.

Up top, Urridge, who was still nattering to Roebuck, peered down circumspectly. 'Hear that, did you?' he asked Roebuck.

Roebuck nodded. 'Yes, I did.'

'Know what it means?'

'Jimmy's for it.'

Urridge gave a snort of derision. 'I'd like to think 'e was!' Urridge was vindictive: he considered he'd been dropped in the crap too often in the past by Jimmy the One, and unjustly – in his own view – at that. 'Just a bollocking in private I reckon – skipper wouldn't do it on the bridge, it's too public like. The lower orders'd get to hear, see?'

'Class and privilege – '

'That's right. And cos o' that Jimmy won't exactly be for it, lad. Skipper'll tear him off a strip I don't doubt – but he won't *do* anything, my arse he won't. Jimmy'll come out right as rain, full o' beans and bounce. The serfs mustn't see officers taken down a peg.' Able Seaman Urridge went to the side of the searchlight platform, closed one nostril with a hammy hand, and blew hard down the other. The result landed on the deck below. 'But we'll *know*, eh?'

'Yes, I suppose so,' Roebuck said. 'Can't do anything about it, though.'

Urridge looked irritated. He disliked having his limitations pointed out. He said, 'That's what you think, lad.'

'Well, what *can* we do?'

'Wait and bloody see,' Urridge said angrily. 'We bide our time, that's what. We bide our time.'

74

Roebuck nodded as though he understood, which he didn't, not wholly anyway. Urridge seemed to be suggesting that they might be able to make use of Jimmy's act of cowardice in some way in the future, and certainly it was true that you should cultivate a good memory for what officers did wrong. There might come a time when the knowledge could be put to productive use, even if you had to wait until after the war when things would change, which was something else Urridge was in the habit of talking a good deal about –

'You there, Urridge.'

Roebuck jumped: the voice was loud and unexpected and it was Petty Officer Jago's.

Urridge looked round. 'Yes, PO?'

'What are you doing up here, then?' Urridge opened his mouth to answer but Jago didn't give him a chance. 'Wardroom pantry's your loafing station, Urridge, and I'll be bound it's in a filthy dirty mess. Get down to it, pronto.'

'I – '

'And don't bloody argue the toss or I'll have you out o' the pantry and cleaning the bilges instead, all right?' Petty Officer Jago stood like a London bobby, hands clasped behind his back, body rising and falling on the balls of his feet. 'And you, Roebuck. What do you happen to be doing?'

'Nothing, PO – '

'Nothing. What an admission – and it's true. Gunner's party – right?'

'Yes,' Roebuck said surlily. The Andrew, he reflected, was full of people who asked you questions they already knew the answers to.

'Don't sound like dumb insolence with me, lad, or you'll get done too. Now – stir yourself. Leading Seaman Prosser, he's detailing hands to assist the Gunner(T) at the tubes. You'll join 'em as an extra seeing as you've nothing else to do. Right – get moving. Belay the last order. Come here.' Jago pushed out his chest. 'I said move, not slouch. Pull your shoulders back and look yuman for a change, why not? Uphill task, but still. God strike a light! What was you in civilian life, might I ask?'

Roebuck clenched his fists. Another question the GI knew the answer to but always waited for Roebuck to put it into words: Roebuck had been a wages clerk in the Landport Drapery Bazaar in Commercial Road in Pompey. Once again, he said so, and Petty Officer Jago savoured it.

'Wish you was there still, I don't doubt.'

'Yes!' Roebuck said between his teeth.

'Yes, GI.'

'Yes, GI.'

'That's better. *Move!*'

Roebuck moved, and moved fast, down the ladder, making for the torpedo-tubes. The destroyer was also moving fast, cutting a swathe through much less turbulent water as she headed on her easterly course towards Burma and the Japanese convoy route from the south. With any luck, Roebuck thought, the needle-in-a-haystack element would come into play and they never would find a convoy. On the other hand, the skipper was always dead keen and the convoy routes were fairly well known, and there was always the radar – a two-edged sword: the enemy radar could pick them up as well.

Roebuck never felt happy until the ship was on her homeward course, if you could call Trincomalee home. To Roebuck home was Pompey and the sooner he got back there the better, though he'd been glad enough to be away from it during the times the bombs and the incendiaries had dropped on it, obliterating Palmerston Road in Southsea, and King's Road, and a large part of the barracks and most of North End. By some miracle his family had been all right; they lived out at Cosham but his mother used to come in shopping and so on, and his father worked in the dockyard itself, travelling backwards and forwards, like all the dockyard mateys, by bicycle, one of thousands pouring in in the morning and out in the evening from the Main Gate on to the Hard or the Unicorn Gate into Edinburgh Road, where the old Coliseum music hall had stood. Roebuck senior had liked going to the Coliseum on Saturday nights after a skinful in the Golden Fleece, but Roebuck's mother had thought it common and so had the other clerks at the Landport Drapery Bazaar. The Coliseum was always full of bluejackets in sweaty serge, largely drunk seamen with groping hands when they sat next to a girl. The Hippodrome, opposite the Theatre Royal, was a class above, and Roebuck sometimes went there with his mother and a young lady from the LDB – Norma Batt. His mum liked Norma Batt because she was polite and did what she was told, and Norma Batt seemed to like Cyril Roebuck's company, a feeling that had not been reciprocated.

Nevertheless, as Roebuck found himself nabbed by Mr Clinch and set to work on the tubes, he thought about Norma Batt, the one girl he had ever known who could be called a girl-friend. Roebuck knew that spots and a scrawny adam's apple and protruding teeth had little sex appeal; it was only the fact that Norma Batt was also so unattractive that had thrown them together – that, and their proximity in the LDB. But now things were different; there was a war on, and he was far from home, and because everyone else had a girl-friend to write to, Roebuck had to have one too.

That was why he had started writing long letters to Norma and getting rather shorter ones back: Norma, now doing war work as a bus conductress, sometimes had late shifts, and weekend shifts. It was also why he had a snapshot to show his messmates, not in fact of Norma, who didn't photograph well, but of a good-looking girl whose name he didn't know – he had found the snapshot in a bus shelter in Greenock on the Clyde and renamed it, for propaganda purposes, Norma. Now, after many, many months of pretence, he was beginning to fancy he was in love with Norma, though when he thought of her at night, in the privacy of his hammock, it was the photograph rather than Norma herself that came mostly to mind. . . .

'You, Roebuck,' Mr Clinch said.

'Yes, sir?'

'Look alive, lad, keep your mind on the job and stop day-dreaming.'

'Yes, sir.'

All thumbs even when he did concentrate. . . . Mr Clinch wondered what the present generation had come to, what the service would come to in the fullness of time, but perhaps you couldn't blame the HO ratings. They hadn't wanted to join.

iii

'You wanted to see me, sir?'

'Yes, Number One. Come in.'

Main came round the door-curtain of Cameron's cabin. Cameron was seated at his desk; he waved the First Lieutenant to a chair in a corner of the cabin. He said, 'I have to make out my report, Number One. On the flooding of the tiller flat.'

'I've already told you – '

'Yes. I know. But so far I've not had the time to draft my own report. And there are certain things that need further investigation.'

'I see.' Main's face had tightened. 'Such as?'

'The casualties, Hanson and Kennet.'

'What about them?'

Cameron said evenly, 'I want to know more precisely how those casualties came about, Number One.'

'But you know that, sir. Gizzard's jamming act, in the hatch.'

'Yes, that's indisputable, of course.' There was still a fairly heavy roll on the destroyer and every now and again she seemed to waggle her stern as though still not happy about the sprung plates. Main was watching the movement of a pencil on the desk, fixing his eyes on its roll as though preferring that to meeting Cameron's stare. 'I'm left wondering why those two were down there, Number One.'

'Someone always has to be last out.'

'Yes. Usually it's the officer or PO in charge. Isn't it?'

78

'So now we know,' Main said truculently. 'You're accusing me of failure to do my duty. Or perhaps of cowardice. You may as well come straight out with it.'

Cameron shook his head. 'At this stage I'm not accusing you of anything – '

'But you've listened to the galley wireless. To gossip.'

'It's any co's job to know what's being said around the ship. But let me finish. I've said I'm not accusing you of anything. But I must have the facts here and now, Number One . . . so that I can decide, decide and write my report for Captain(D).' The cabin was hot, stifling; sweat poured down Cameron's face and arms. 'The first thing I want to know is this: do you, with hindsight, consider that perhaps you left the order too late? The order to clear the tiller flat?'

'I was – yes, possibly I did. I was relying on Kennet, you see.'

'Relying on your petty officer?'

'It's normal,' Main said. 'They're reliable men – usually.'

'I agree. But you don't rely on your PO to give the order to clear a compartment. That's your job.'

'Kennet seemed to know . . . I expected him to give me a warning. He didn't. He left it too late. It wasn't my fault.'

Cameron said icily, 'Don't lay the blame on a dead man, Number One. That won't wash with me. I'm taking it you're admitting you were slow to appreciate the danger and to take action in time. Well, that's a question of judgment, of course, but the fact remains that you can't make an excuse of it. As officers, we stand or fall by our judgment, which has to be right.'

Main flared up. 'Oh, don't sound so bloody sanctimonious! Don't you realize you're talking to someone who was at Dartmouth, that I'm RN whereas you – '

'That's enough,' Cameron said. He got to his feet. After a moment the First Lieutenant also got up. His face was as white as a sheet and his eyes were blazing, his fists clenched. Then, unexpectedly, he apologized.

'I'm sorry, sir. That was unforgivable. After all . . . you are the Captain.'

Cameron nodded. 'I accept your apology, Number One. A deaf ear this time. But my report will indicate what you've said in regard to the tiller flat. And there's one more thing, potentially much more serious. I want to know why you were on the safe side of the hatch when those men died in what had become a trap.'

'You mean we're back to cowardice.'

'No. I'm only asking for your explanation. Once I've had it – then we'll see.'

Main began talking; something about it being his duty to take overall charge . . . but he hadn't got far when he was interrupted by the whistle of Cameron's voice-pipe. From the bridge Pegram reported: there was smoke distantly, on the horizon to the south-east.

7

CAMERON and Main went fast up the ladders to the forebridge. Cameron picked up the smoke, studied it through his binoculars. 'More than one ship, that's for sure, Pegram. Radar?'

'Nothing, sir. Not in range yet.'

'No.' Just a routine query: the ships were still hull down, the smoke the only give-away. 'You've been taking bearings, Pegram?'

'Yes, sir. They're drawing to port. Slowly but surely!'

'Which means they're heading north,' Cameron said. He brought his binoculars down and glanced across at Dawnay. 'What d'you think, Pilot?'

'I think it's a convoy,' Dawnay answered.

'So do I. I'm going to work on that assumption. Number One?'

'Sir?'

'I'm going to second degree of readiness rather than action stations for the time being. I intend to turn away – keep out of sight during daylight hours – but I'll come back to a parallel course when I'm far enough west and increase speed so as to keep ahead of the convoy. I shall go to normal dusk action stations, and after full dark I'll turn towards the convoy's course, and cut down on them from the north. The ship's to be in all respects ready for action by the time I make the turn. All right?'

'I'll see to it, sir.' The First Lieutenant paused. 'There's the question of damage-control parties.'

'Yes.' During the hurricane Cameron had wanted the First Lieutenant aft in the tiller flat, taking charge of what would have been the emergency steering position; in action the considerations were different. The First Lieutenant would be needed around the decks, in general charge rather than confined to one station, to be available wherever his authority might be required – if only to take over the command if Cameron should be killed. Cameron said, 'Normal action requirements, Number One. I take it the ERA can cope?'

Main said yes, he could. As the First Lieutenant left the bridge there was a curious constriction in the air and Cameron believed that both the navigator and Pegram felt it as well as he. Main's question, basically an unnecessary one, had been loaded, as though he were sounding the Captain out following the interview so recently interrupted below. If so, he would now be none the wiser. As Cameron passed the order to take the *Caithness* westerly for a while and then alter back to a course parallel to the enemy convoy, he tried without success to cast all anxiety about the First Lieutenant from his mind. Before being interrupted earlier by the voice-pipe from the bridge Main had said something about it being his duty to take overall charge and the best way of doing that was, in his view, to be on the other side of the hatch so as to supervise the emergence of the damage-control party. If the spirit of Petty Officer Kennet had happened to be hovering in the vicinity when Main said that, he would have congratulated himself on having made an accurate forecast of just what Jimmy *would* say to the skipper. Cameron, in ignorance of Kennet's last thoughts on earth, came to the same conclusion: it was just what he would have expected Main to say. And, of course, though Cameron believed there had in fact been other considerations to sway his First Lieutenant's decision, he had to concede that there was some sense in it. For the officer in charge to be hemmed in down below while the rest scrambled clear didn't give that officer much chance to take charge. It was fifty-fifty; and Cameron was coming to the conclusion that there was little he could do about it. He would report the facts as established, the plain unvarnished facts, and then it would be up to Captain(D). It would be grossly unfair of him to offer any opinion that would brand Main as a coward in the absence of any hard proof.

That left the ship's company. What were they going to think, what construction would they place on no action apparently being taken? The senior ratings would of course understand that any action taken would be taken invisibly as it were, a mere matter of reports that could lead to Main being relieved at the first opportunity and possibly facing court martial later. Not so the younger ones. Cameron would have to rely upon the good sense of the senior men to keep the air as clear as possible. There was one way of fanning the flames, and Cameron was well aware that he had already taken it: action requirements or not, plenty of ratings were going to read quite a lot into Main not being in charge again in the tiller flat. That was unfair to Main himself, but there was the element of the cleft stick. Any other considerations apart, Cameron was certainly not going to risk Main going into a repeat performance. . . .

Command was a lonely state: there was no one with whom Cameron could talk things out, no one whose conversation and point of view could help him towards decision – not in a matter of this kind. Officers who commanded ships had to be self-reliant and needed plenty of self-confidence to bolster it. They also had to have thick skins, yet not thick enough to be entirely insensitive to the human condition. They needed the wisdom of Solomon, and by the nature of their appointments they were God as well.

With a further effort Cameron forced Main from his mind. But not very far: there would have to be a briefing, his intentions for the forthcoming action made known to his officers and senior ratings. He swung round on Pegram. 'Send down to the First Lieutenant and all heads of departments. Muster in my cabin in fifteen minutes. Get Ringrose to relieve you on the bridge.' Cameron grinned. 'How's the link with the Almighty?'

'In contact, sir.'

'Signals good?'

'There's encouragement around, I think.'

'I'm glad to hear it. Put in a word for the rest of us, won't you?'

ii

Pegram knew that his guns were good; so were his guns' crews, mostly, though there was a lack of experience among the junior ratings, some of whom had joined as replacements last time in Trincomalee. Petty Officer Jago had licked them into shape so far as possible, but he hadn't had enough time, thanks largely to the hurricane, to do a fully satisfactory job. Because the success of the attack depended on the guns, the rest of the day was spent in exercising action, again and again and again until Cameron, Pegram and Petty Officer Jago were satisfied. Cameron's idea, expounded when the muster had taken place in his cabin, was to cut across the convoy escort at maximum speed, with all guns firing, sink or disable the leader, and then turn to deal with the escorts on the flanks. He could not, of course, expect too much of the element of surprise: the inward rush of the *Caithness* would be picked up by the enemy radar, that was inevitable.

'And what after that, sir?' Mr Clinch asked, looking highly doubtful of any success at all. 'Suppose we *do* sink the whole perishing escort – '

'Don't let us suppose anything, Torps. We're *going* to sink them. The chances are there'll be only the one destroyer, backed up by smaller escort vessels – don't forget, the Japs feel safe in this area. And after that, well, we turn the merchant ships westerly and herd them into Trinco. That's all. That's if there are British prisoners of war aboard.'

Main asked, 'And if not?'

'If not, we sink them too. I'm not forgetting the likelihood

of opposition on the way back. I intend to draft a cypher for
c-in-c telling him what I'm doing and asking for a surface
force to meet us, with air support if possible. That'll be sent
out, in fact, the moment we're in contact with the convoy.
Because from then on, there'll be no point in maintaining w/T
silence. Any other questions?'

'Yes, sir,' the Gunner(T) said. 'What about my torpedoes?'

'Have them on the top line, Torps. I'll be using them just as
soon as I need to, to back up the guns.'

There was a faint stir between the Gunner(T) and the GI. Mr
Clinch disliked hearing his tubes referred to as a mere back-
up; Petty Officer Jago didn't think his guns needed any back-
up at all. They were more than capable on their own. Walking
away from the Captain's cabin when the muster broke up,
Jago moved along the decks to his guns, fore and aft and
amidships, continuing the interrupted gun-drill, making sure
that no cack-handed gunnery rate was going to let him down.

iii

Aboard the Navy's smaller war vessels it was customarily the
Surgeon Lieutenant's job to deal with the encyphering and
decyphering of signals. In all conscience the doctor had little
else to do; the men of a ship's company were healthy animals
and largely the MO was there as an action requirement:
emergency operations, wounds, injections of pain-killing
drugs. He could be busy enough once the guns opened but
when not in action he was available for the odd jobs as they
cropped up. The message that had come to him from the
bridge for encyphering was a fairly long one. Styles wasn't all
that fast with the cyphering and recyphering tables and as he
worked away at the message he had a lot on his mind. For one
thing there was the Jap: both Cameron and Styles had
questioned the man again, putting to him the theory of British
prisoners of war being transported; he had refused to answer
anything and throughout the questioning had kept an
expressionless face, so nothing had been gleaned from his

reactions. Another worry was the First Lieutenant, and his attitude to what Cameron was doing.

Main had approached the doctor for aspirins. He had a foul headache, he said. As a routine measure Styles had taken his temperature: it was normal. He'd parted with a couple of aspirins and then Number One had started a bellyache about the Captain.

'It's crazy,' he said.

Styles looked up. 'What is?'

'Going into an attack single-handed.'

'We haven't got anyone else to help us, have we? What do you suggest he ought to do?'

Main said, 'He ought to leave it.'

'Turn for home?'

'Yes. What he's doing is against the spirit of c-in-c's orders. Orders not to engage unless forced to. We're on patrol, that's all. Observe and report.'

Styles noted the shake in Main's fingers as he lit a cigarette. He said mildly, 'There's the British troops. Or so Cameron believes. If he can bring it off – '

'He hasn't a hope!'

'If he can bring it off,' Styles went on doggedly, 'it'll be something to boost morale out here. Vian of the *Cossack* again,' he added in reference to the boarding of the prison ship *Altmark* in Norwegian waters. 'We need a bit of that . . . and there's the troops themselves, of course. Being in the hands of the Japs isn't – '

'I've just said . . . he hasn't a hope.'

'Why not?'

Main took a deep breath. 'One bloody destroyer, Doc! It's lunacy. The merchant ships'll be armed for a start, leave alone the escort. If there's any air cover around – '

'Will there be, d'you think?'

Main shrugged. 'I don't know. I suppose it's probably unlikely the Japs would see a need, considering they have total command of the area – '

'Except for us. We're here, sticking our nose in. The Japs aren't all that hot.'

Main spread his hands and said, 'You don't understand. You just don't understand any more than Cameron does. You're a medic, it's not your job to understand. Cameron's RNVR. Saturday-afternoon sailors we used to call them.'

'We've done more than Saturday afternoons for a good few years now, Number One. Don't forget I'm RNVR too.'

'It's different for doctors. You're a doctor wherever you go. Cameron calls himself an executive officer. He's fighting a war – I'm not saying he hasn't done well – '

'Glad to hear it! His DSC speaks for that.'

'Yes. But he hasn't had the experience, the experience to make decisions of this sort, life and death for a whole ship's company.'

Styles asked politely, 'Have *you*?'

Main flushed. 'I'm RN. I've had the training. Four years at Dartmouth to begin with. You're moulded to a way of thought. When the time comes, you react to that. You make the right decisions.'

'Which aren't always the easy ones, I'd say. I think Cameron has guts. It won't be the first time someone's gone in against all the odds. Take Kennedy of the *Rawalpindi*. He was RN. And he went in single-handed against a Jerry battle-cruiser. He had guts too.'

That was when Main turned away, angrily and with a face gone suddenly white. Styles, as he worked away at the signal, wondered if he'd gone too far. His tone, he knew, had been cold and it must have been fairly obvious that he was suggesting a lack of personal guts on the part of the First Lieutenant. Anyway, it was too late now. He'd said what he said and the *Caithness* was committed whether or not Main was happy about it. Styles couldn't deny that he had his own fears for the immediate future: it was going to be very, very dicey. But when you were at war you had to accept the risks, and you had to do your duty. Duty was to some people an old-fashioned concept, or at any rate the word itself was. It reeked of past glories and selfless actions and one used it self-consciously, almost in inverted commas. But there had been so many men within living memory who had regarded it highly. Sir Christopher Cradock, engaging the Germans off Coronel in 1914 with his outdated, almost useless squadron; Evans of the old destroyer *Broke* who, when with the Dover Patrol, sank two U-boats on one occasion, one by ramming, the other by torpedo attack . . . and in this war not only Vian and Kennedy but Fogarty Fegen in the armed merchant cruiser *Jervis Bay*; Lord Louis Mountbatten in the *Kelly*; Lieutenant-Commander Esmonde leading his old stringbags, the Swordfish aircraft of the Fleet Air Arm, against the Channel dash of the *Scharnhorst* and the *Gneisenau*; Williamson who had led the air strike at Taranto. Cameron, right or wrong, was in very good company.

But it wasn't only the First Lieutenant who had doubts. There was a good deal of muttering along the messdecks and at the guns and tubes. It was something like a fifty-fifty split: incipient hero, or lunatic out for glory. In Stripey Gizzard's view both terms came to the same thing. Heroes were the ones who'd had more than their fair share of luck and so were the lunatics who'd managed to survive. You called them heroes when it was all over but you didn't think about the men who'd died to put them on their pinnacle. Casualties, they said, were inevitable in war. So why have a war?

Gizzard, thinking about that one, slowly scratched at his stomach. In action he would be back in the tiller flat. He was, frankly, terrified at the prospect, seeing his gut getting all jammed up again if there was another emergency. It wasn't fair to put him there, not with his stomach. . . .

He had mentioned this to the 'swain, just in case Chapman hadn't thought about it. The 'swain had charge of the Watch and Quarter Bill, but was busy when Gizzard put his viewpoint and all he'd said had been, 'Slim it down, then.'

Gizzard had been indignant. 'Wot, between now and – '

'Hop it, Gizzard.'

'That's all very well, 'Swain, but – '

'For God's sake, I'm not mucking up the whole bloody shoot just on account of your stomach. Next time you're ashore, lay off the chips. For now, bugger off.'

The skipper had a lot to answer for, Gizzard thought angrily. By now they should be on their way back to base, and all that crumpet on offer in Trinco . . . beer, and big eats, and crumpet made up Gizzard's shore-side life. The activity required when dealing with crumpet ought by rights to help slim the stomach, but it was heavily outdone by the big eats and the beer. You couldn't win.

iv

Ordinary Seaman Roebuck found himself buttonholed by Able Seaman Urridge in the afternoon watch when the hands had been piped yet again to exercise action. Urridge believed he had something to get his teeth into. Sidling up, he spoke from the corner of his mouth.

'Got away with it 'e did.'

'Who? What?'

'Bloody Jimmy. Buzz says, 'e got a bit of a bollocking and that's all. Like I predicted.'

'Ar.'

Urridge looked impatient. 'It's all very well just saying ar. Point is, it bears out what I said earlier – '

'Class and privilege?'

Urridge nodded. 'That's right, lad, class and privilege. Anyone else, they'd get shot. Not officers. Get away with murder. Talking of murder,' he added after a pause.

'What?'

'This bloody antic the skipper's on. Heading for the Japs. When the 'istory of the war comes to be written like, know what they'll say, do you?'

'No,' Roebuck said, looking keen to learn.

'They'll say it was *all* murder. All them blokes what led matlows and brown jobs and even the bleedin' Brylcreem

Boys to their deaths . . . murderers the lot of 'em, they'll say – 'istory will say that, like.'

'Depends who writes it,' Roebuck said.

'Well,' Urridge conceded, 'there's that an' all. But truth will out, I reckon. Things is going to be different when this lot's over, which I may 'ave said before now.'

'Yes.'

'But in the meantime, see, the skipper's intent on getting well in with the bloody brass and never mind what 'appens to us. That's not right and no one can say it is – and you needn't remind me about them pongoes, if they exist at all. It's all bloody guesswork, Japs transporting British troops! Sticking our necks out for a fairy story, we are!'

'Nothing we can do about it,' Roebuck said. 'Not short of mutiny.'

Urridge sucked in his cheeks. 'Don't use that word, lad,' he said sharply. 'Get us shot, that will.'

Roebuck nodded and thought about the awful consequences of mutiny. Part of his reading matter since being conscripted into the Navy had been the Articles of War. They were full of doom, laying down the punishment scales for miscreants, and virtually all of them itemized death as being the appropriate punishment, though mostly this was then watered down to 'or such other punishment as may be hereinafter mentioned'. But for mutiny, death was obligatory. Of course, it could only be awarded by court martial in normal circumstances, but Roebuck fancied he had read somewhere that a captain had the right when at sea, if he considered it necessary in the interest of maintaining discipline in action, to administer the death penalty there and then. Off his own bat as it were. Policeman, judge, jury, executioner, undertaker, the lot. And not much chance of appeal.

'You there, Roebuck.'

Roebuck jumped. Petty Officer Jago again: Ginger Jago, dead keen, all for it, as pusser as the bar of yellow soap which was the only sort of soap you ever got from the paymaster's stores, all gas and gaiters like any other gunner's mate. Roebuck said, 'Yes, GI?'

'Talking to yourself, first sign of insanity – ask the quack. Don't mutter. Concentrate on the gun. What's on your mind to mutter about, eh? That's if you've got a mind. Well?'

'Yes, I've got a mind,' Roebuck said. Fury rose in him: bloody Jago would never have the brains to work for the Landport Drapery Bazaar. But to say as much to Jago might well be to sound like a mutineer.

Jago stood there like a brick wall, staring. 'So answer my question. You've got a mind, according to you. What's on it?'

Roebuck squeezed out some inspiration, heaven sent. 'I was repeating the misfire drill, GI. To myself, see.'

'Oh-ah. Very bright I'm sure.' Jago looked as though he were about to tell Roebuck to repeat it aloud, but Roebuck was in luck: Jago was already switching his attention to Able Seaman Urridge, now on deck by right. In action, and when exercising action, Urridge's station was loading number on Two gun, and as such he was released from his duties as wardroom messman for all gun drills.

Jago looked Urridge up and down and seemed unimpressed with what he saw. He said, 'Don't look too happy, do you?'

'Oh, I dunno, GI – '

'I do! Try to look happier, even if it's only pretend, eh? Happy gun's crew makes a happy gun, and a happy gun fires better – right?'

'Right, GI.' To himself Urridge said, 'Bollocks.'

'Glad you agree. Best foot foremost when we picks up the Nip convoy or I'll be having your guts for garters. You've got enough fat.' Jago prodded Urridge in the stomach. 'Bad as that Gizzard, you are. Comes of eating up all the wardroom gash, I s'pose.'

Urridge gave a sycophantic grin: talk about wit, but it was dangerous to answer back. Jago went on his way, spreading keenness around all the action positions. Gun drill occupied the rest of the afternoon watch, Lieutenant Pegram co-ordinating the exercise in the director above the bridge with his director layer, Leading Seaman Prosser. Prosser was feeling fed up, ballsed up and far from home and he was going through the motions of director laying automatically and with only half his mind on the job. Married a year ago to the day, just a week before getting his draft chit out East, and not seen his wife since. The last mail back in Trinco had brought word that Ivy had a bun in the oven. It wasn't Ivy who'd written, it was his mother, never slow to announce bad news though this time she did it out of a sense of duty: her Barry ought to know what was going on while he was serving the King . . . Prosser had almost heard the tongue clicks. Mum had been circum-spect: she hadn't used the expression bun in the oven, of course; Ivy, she wrote, was 'carrying'. She hinted at a leading writer from the Pay Office in Pompey barracks, a name unknown to Leading Seaman Prosser but anyone in the writer branch was a smoothie and a fat-arsed clerk. Mum was terribly sorry for him – for her son, not the leading writer – and that made Prosser mad. He knew mum was probably relishing it all, since she'd never had any time for Ivy, called her a tart. Now she'd been proved right, anyway in her own eyes. Prosser, as he listened to Lieutenant Pegram's orders and moved dials and switches and followed pointers in his cramped position, was still composing the letter he would have to write to Ivy. He had yet to sort out his reactions. Blame or understanding? It wasn't all roses back in Pompey, a wife all on her own with all the temptations and all the bombs and that. He'd have liked to talk to someone about it, an old mate perhaps, but he'd not been long in the *Caithness*, drafted from the pool in Trinco as a casualty replacement, and he hadn't what you could call old mates. He could put in a request to see his divisional officer, who happened to be Lieutenant Pegram. Pegram seemed a decent bloke. Maybe he would do that. Or maybe it didn't matter: when they picked up that convoy they might all be blown out of the water.

92

Exercise action drew to a close at eight bells and the guns' crews were stood down except for half the armament which remained manned in second degree of readiness. Prosser went down to the mess for a cup of char and a thick slice of bread with pusser's strawberry jam out of what looked a giant-sized paint tin. Jago marched along to the petty officers' mess where he moaned about the bloody ineptitude of the hostilities-only men. Chief PO Bustacle, chief boatswain's mate, added a couple of paragraphs to a letter to his wife: he wrote something every day at sea, all things being equal, and then posted the screed in Trincomalee on return to harbour. Yeoman of Signals Venner took over on the flag deck, relieving his leading signalman and worrying about a mysterious boil that had appeared on his backside a couple of days out of Trinco. Like Gizzard, like so many of them, crumpet loomed large in Venner's life when away from home and boils were always suspicious; but so far he hadn't gone near the quack. Couldn't face the possible verdict, so he'd spread himself liberally with Germolene and was hoping for the best. He told himself it was a combination of the vicious heat and the rotten diet but at the same time thanked God he wasn't married.

Cameron, hunched as usual in the fore part of the bridge, watched the going down of the sun towards what was to be a brilliant and spectacular sunset. After that, the swift tropical dark closed in and the stars came out. The weather was near perfect now, all trace of the hurricane's after effects suddenly gone. The *Caithness* steamed through an almost flat sea, rolling gently to what was left of the swell, cutting a swathe of phosphorescence through the dark water, no lights showing and the men of the watch on deck relaxing as they waited for the order that would send them to their destiny.

The time for the alteration came when the onset of the dark was complete. Cameron said quietly, 'Right, Pilot.'

'Aye, aye, sir.' Dawnay took the ship over from the officer of the watch and bent to the voice-pipe. 'Starboard ten,' he ordered.

The quartermaster responded. 'Starboard ten, sir.' A pause as the telemotor steering gear turned over. 'Ten of starboard wheel on, sir.' The destroyer began swinging.

Dawnay watched the gyro repeater in the binnacle, dimly glowing. 'Steady!'

'Steady, sir. Course, oh nine oh degrees, sir.'

'Steer that.'

'Steer oh nine oh, sir.'

The navigator reported to the shadowy figure ahead of him. 'On course, sir, to cross ahead of the convoy.'

Cameron looked round briefly. 'Thank you, Pilot. ETA?'

'First light, sir: 0400.'

'Right.' Cameron came away from his stool and took up the Tannoy. He flicked it on. He said, 'This is the Captain . . . hands will be piped to action stations at 0330 hours unless we've had to close up earlier, which I don't expect. We have now altered eastwards to cut across the convoy, which I expect to pick up at around 0400. For now, that's all. I shall keep the ship's company informed of any developments.'

The Tannoy clicked off. On the upper deck, down by the tubes, Mr Clinch pushed his cap to the back of his head and said, 'Now, what does he mean by that, eh? Can't be any developments, I reckon, except what we'll all be able to hear for ourselves. Or maybe he's thinking of signal traffic, incoming messages. . . .'

He was talking to his leading torpedoman, Charlie Inman. The LTO said they all knew as much as the next man and that wasn't worth writing home about. Inman was making a few checks on the tubes; Mr Clinch hung about for a while, watching him. Then he decided to take the opportunity to turn in for a spell. But he found sleep didn't come and never mind how tired he was after the hurricane and all. In the early hours, the middle watch, he gave it up and went on deck to look up at the stars, as if they might have some useful buzz. He paced the deck; he had a feeling something was about to happen, he didn't know why. He'd been pacing up and down for quite a while when he heard it: the sound of aircraft engines, distant but closing from the east.

8

THE RADAR cabinet reported to the bridge: unidentified aircraft, six in number, coming in low. In the starlit Indian Ocean night the *Caithness* would stand out like a sore thumb. The incoming aircraft had the sound of something heavy. Cameron called to the yeoman of signals.

'Stand by with the identification signal, Yeoman.'

'Aye, aye, sir.' Venner was ready with his Aldis lamp, angling it into the sky. Seconds later the shapes could be seen flitting across the stars. They were hard to identify but Cameron fancied they were torpedo-bombers – could be Japanese but equally could be American, perhaps from a carrier somewhere in the Indian Ocean or the Bay of Bengal. They were coming lower to investigate: *Caithness* had been seen. Cameron passed the order to Venner, who made the identification signal of the day. From the leader a light flashed back, and Venner reported: 'Correct reply, sir.'

Cameron blew out a breath of relief. He said, 'Call them again, Yeoman. Tell 'em I have a message.'

'Aye, aye, sir.' Venner used his Aldis again, received a response. The aircraft – they were in fact USN bombers – banked and started circling the destroyer. Cameron passed his message: he was heading for the convoy route and expected to be in action soon after dawn. He would appreciate support from Trincomalee. The reply came back that his message would be passed on after the aircraft were

96

back at base. And in the meantime the leader had news for Cameron: he had carried out an attack on a northbound convoy and had sunk two escorts, one big merchant ship and a smaller one. The attack had been broken off when the aviation spirit had got too low for comfort. He passed the convoy's last known position, then resumed his course for base, and the sounds died away westwards.

Dawnay said with much satisfaction, 'That makes our job easier – two escorts gone!'

'If it's the same convoy we're after. Probably it is.'

'It's good news anyway. The sailors are going to like this, sir.' Dawnay paused. 'No indication where they're from. Those aircraft.'

'Never mind, they're history now, Pilot. I just hope they get that message through, that's all.'

'If they do,' Dawnay said, 'we may be pulled out. Ordered back to Trinco.'

'We may, but I doubt it. Trinco'll want that convoy finished off, routine patrol orders or not – now a blow's been struck –'

'Yes, point taken, but I'm not so sure it's going to be easier after all. The Japs'll be sending replacements to take the convoy over, escorts from Rangoon or Java or Sumatra. A long way, but it's a case of who gets there first.' Dawnay was speaking over his shoulder: he was already laying off a course more directly for the convoy's position as reported by the aircraft. A moment later he straightened and turned. He said, 'I suggest we alter five degrees south. The convoy's not as far north as I'd estimated, sir. If we alter, we should pick them up a little earlier.'

'Do that, Pilot. And engines to full ahead. And just in case, we'll go to first degree of readiness now.'

ii

Cameron spoke once again to his ship's company, putting them in the picture. There was cheering when he announced the air attack on the convoy. There was a sense of urgency now, a race against time. The *Caithness* had something over thirty-two knots available on full power and Cameron expected to make contact with the convoy within two hours. So far, so good; but it was to be expected that the Japs would now send out cover for the convoy. Indeed, aircraft might already be circling, a protective umbrella over the merchant ships.

Below in his engine-room, Mr Henty felt the surge of power being transmitted to the shafts. The whole compartment throbbed and pulsed and Henty wiped streaming sweat from his face with a handful of cotton-waste. Chief ERA Trigg moved around, watching, feeling bearings, thrusting the long neck of an oil can in here and there. In the boiler room Stoker PO Tallis kept a sharp eye on his dials and gauges, watched the white heat behind the boiler plates, and wondered what it would be like to be cremated alive if anything untoward, like a Jap projy, penetrated the thin steel sides of the destroyer and entered the boiler room. It would probably all be over pretty quick, of course, but there must be at least a moment when you knew what was happening and felt the terrible searing heat as the oil fuel and the fires burst out from the boilers. In the engine-room itself they would face a different death from being boiled in escaping steam, which, under intense pressure, would peel away the skin in seconds, leaving all hands like lobsters, raw and red. Tallis felt a good deal of envy for the men in the exposed positions on the upper deck, on the bridge, at the guns and torpedo-tubes. Up there they had a better chance. . . .

Tallis was a man of imagination and he could see it all. He saw it every time when action was imminent. He dreamed about it, too, on occasions, and woke sweating and trembling. It had become worse, much worse, after Grace and the kids had got it. Grace and their two daughters, Doreen and Sally, aged five and eight, had been burned to death when the Nazis had come over Devonport and dropped HE and incendiaries. The little house – something had drawn him to go and look at it when he'd got compassionate leave from his ship in Rosyth

– had been a shell like all the rest of the street, gaunt, blackened and utterly pathetic. Tallis had recalled it as last he had seen it: a neat little garden in front, Grace's pride and joy. She had anticipated each spring, right through the winter days, waiting for the clump of forsythia to spread its yellow flowers in welcome. A house of laughter and bright decorations, all gone now.

Tallis had talked to a man he'd known, an occasional drinking companion in his local, which was still there though looking worn and paint-peeled. This man was in the Auxiliary Fire Service, and he'd been there when Tallis' house had gone. It was all over very quick, he said, they wouldn't have suffered long. The heat had been intense and no one could get near. The rescue services had been stretched in any case. Because of that imagination of his, Tallis had seen his family, scorched, blackened, crisped. After that, his nightmares had brought them back to him in that state, time after time until he believed he must go mad.

'All right, Tallis?'

Tallis turned, with a start; the warrant engineer had come through from the engine-room. 'All right, sir, yes.'

'All bearing an equal strain, as they say.'

'That's right.' Tallis hesitated, then asked, 'What do you make of it all, sir?'

'Make of it? I dunno, really. Bit of a fool's errand, I reckon. Just us, just one bloody ship! But the fact the skipper's asked for assistance . . . makes a difference, does that.'

'Not much time, is there?'

Henty said, 'Not for surface support, no. They may send aircraft, though. Let's hope so, anyway.' He turned away and went back to the engine-room, resuming his position on the starting platform. He was thinking about Stoker PO Tallis and the loss he had sustained. The personal tragedy wasn't unique, of course, it was one of thousands that the war had brought, but that fact didn't do anything to lessen it for Tallis. Henty had an idea Tallis wouldn't mind being blown to Kingdom Come and a chance of meeting his family again.

Henty, whose own wife was safe and sound down in Dorset – so far as he knew, and he crossed his fingers as the thought came to him – pondered on that particular chance. Himself, he wouldn't have set a lot of store by it. When you died, you died and that was it – finish. Nothing left anywhere except within the confines of a grave if you survived the war at sea to die ashore. Other people had other views: Mr Pegram for one. Henty had yarned about it with Pegram from time to time, for Pegram had religion and liked to spread the gospel so long as he had a willing listener, though he never actually plugged it. He was convinced of an after life and of a rendezvous in a better place. He didn't convince Henty but at least he was happy himself in his belief and Henty was willing to concede that any belief must be good if it removed the fear of death, which it had done in Pegram's case – he wasn't in the least worried by danger. Often Mr Henty wished that he to had a belief . . . and standing there on the starting platform, steaming at full power towards God knew what, he realized with something of a shock that that was precisely what the devil-dodgers said was the first step towards getting one.

iii

In the w/t office Petty Officer Telegraphist Potts was keeping a listening watch, headphones clamped over his sandy head, fingers delicately making adjustments to his knobs and dials. There was a good deal of interference: probably due to the hurricane, still whirling around somewhere to the north-east. There was plenty of radio traffic but nothing of any consequence to *Caithness*. As he listened his eyes roved: Leading Telegraphist Flannery had been at it again, changing over his pin-ups. Big bare buttocks stared down at Potts, a nude with hands on her hips, glancing over her shoulder from beneath a fuzz of blonde hair. Next to her was a girl facing front and equally naked, with tits like balloons and one leg lifted, the foot resting against the opposite knee.

Good, clean fun no doubt, Potts thought sardonically, but

100

knew that in fact Flannery was sex mad. One night ashore and he came back aboard looking like the wreck of the *Hesperus*. And his stock of pin-ups was apparently inexhaustible; he seemed to change them every time the bell struck. Potts had expressed disapproval but hadn't given any order for their removal. He liked to run a happy department and Flannery was a first-class leading hand in every other way. Flannery was there now, keeping the listening watch – Potts was merely monitoring, and he removed his headphones to ease away a slight headache. He thought about the aircraft, and the signals that had been passed by lamp.

When they got back to base the aircraft leader would pass Cameron's message to c-in-c. In Potts' view that meant the aircraft were not from a carrier: no carrier would break wireless silence at sea to pass a message. So if they were based on Ceylon, there might well be a response to the message before the *Caithness* made contact with the convoy. Those planes should be back at base inside a couple of hours and c-in-c would obviously recognize the urgency and wouldn't be wasting any time.

Potts looked up, past the nudes in their poses, at the clock on the bulkhead in front of him: one hour and ten minutes since the contact with the aircraft. By now the *Caithness* couldn't be far off the convoy. Potts found sweat pouring from his face and he mopped with a handkerchief. Already twice a survivor from destroyers that had bought it, Potts didn't want to have to swim a third time. He didn't believe his luck would extend that far. For one thing, there were sharks in these waters.

Potts rubbed at his eyes and then put his headphones back on. As he did so there was a change, a sudden easing of the vibration brought to the ship by the use of full power, and the deck of the w/t office heeled over to port. Then the vibration ceased.

They had stopped. A moment later there was a heavy juddering as the engines were put astern. Everything shook:

one of the nudes came adrift and fluttered down on to the transmit key at Potts' right hand.

Flannery said, 'What the sod.'

'We're going astern,' Potts said.

'Sure we're going astern, PO. Why?'

Potts shrugged. He pushed irritably at the fallen nude. Flannery said, 'Hands off her arse, if you don't mind.'

iv

There were four lifeboats, laden with men and linked together by grass lines, one ahead of the other. The starboard lookout had been the first to spot them, as he swept his arc with his binoculars. Cameron had picked them up, broad on the starboard bow, and had at once put his engines astern and turned towards them. As the sternway checked his speed he passed the order down to stop, and the *Caithness* drifted slowly towards the boats as her way came off. It was fairly obvious the boats were from the convoy, following the aircraft attack.

Cameron moved to the after part of the bridge and called down to the upper deck.

'Number One. . . '

'Here, sir.' The voice was right below him: Main was at the foot of the bridge ladder.

'Stand by to grapple the boats in, Number One. Starboard side aft. Have a party ready with rifles – report when they've mustered. I'll hold off until then.'

'You think they'll open fire, sir?'

Cameron gave a hard laugh. 'I'm not taking chances, anyway!' He studied the boats through his binoculars: the low-hanging stars added to the moon's light gave him a fair view. He believed he saw British Army uniforms, khaki drill, but couldn't be sure. What he was sure of was that there were Japanese Army caps, and there was the positive glint of steel – bayonets at the ends of rifles. From the look of it there were

102

men sick or wounded or both. A number of bodies lay in awkward positions and had a listless look about them as the boats drifted closer. Cameron was to some extent puzzled that the Japs weren't making a run for it. Surrender wasn't normally their line, but maybe simple prudence was: they hadn't much hope of evading a destroyer, that was certain.

Main passed the armed guard order to Petty Officer Jago, and Jago rustled up the hands in double-quick time. 'You and you and you, look lively, draw rifles, ten in number. Bring 'em back here fast.' He detailed seven more seamen to fall in on the side away from the lifeboats and wait for the rifles. One of them was Ordinary Seaman Burden, another was Able Seaman Urridge, another Urridge's mate Roebuck. Roebuck's teeth were chattering, warm though the night was. Roebuck hadn't yet met the enemy face to face but he'd heard a lot about Jap brutality and Jap tenacity. Waiting for the rifle issue, he tried to dream up an excuse for falling out but couldn't think of anything in the least likely to convince Petty Officer Jago.

Jago, however, could read minds. Or so it was popularly believed. Now, Jago offered proof of his powers.

He stopped in his up-and-down march and confronted Roebuck. 'You, Roebuck. Shit scared by the look of you. Right?'

'Course not, PO – '

Jago said, 'Nothing to be scared of. We're bigger than them!'

'They've got guns – '

'So've we.'

Roebuck didn't say any more. No point, not with Jago, the sod. But he knew the Japs weren't going to submit to being taken prisoner and there would be a bloodbath when they opened fire. Glancing for'ard towards the bridge, Roebuck saw that the close-range weapons – machine-guns, pom-poms abaft the funnel, Oerlikons – were trained on the lifeboats. That was comforting but Roebuck knew there would be dilemma on the bridge. Like Cameron, he had seen what he

103

believed to be British uniforms. It would be impossible to open fire without killing the prisoners of war, who made a handy shield for the Japs.

9

AMONG THE SURVIVORS from the convoy escort was Commander Kuroda, lately of the flotilla leader *Oita*, now sunk as a result of the brutal attack by aircraft. Commander Kuroda was very bitter: had the convoy not been delayed by engine trouble aboard one of the merchant ships, it might not have run into those aircraft, which Commander Kuroda believed had come upon the convoy by the sheerest chance. Naturally, the convoy routes were known to the British and Americans but the dates and times of the sailings were not, or should not be, and in fact the convoys had never before come under attack. However, they had caused him personal ruin. When the war was won, he would be dishonoured – not by having bravely lost his ship, but by being, as now seemed likely, taken prisoner.

His Emperor did not like prisoners. Neither did Kuroda's senior officers, nor indeed did anyone else in Nippon.

From where he sat in the sternsheets of the leading lifeboat, Commander Kuroda, small and wizened, bright-eyed with hate for the British, studied the angle of the close-range weapons, their barrels pointing down to cover the boats. The British were capable of anything and might well open fire, even upon their own men . . . and by this time the lifeboats were coming very close to the British destroyer, bringing it well within the range of Kuroda's rifles if he should decide to use them.

What would his Emperor expect of him?

Not cowardice, certainly. That was not to be thought of.

It was clear enough, really: he must fight, he must use such weapons as he had, however useless, however pitiful they might be against the gun-power of a destroyer. As Commander Kuroda came to his feet to call the orders across the water to his linked flotilla of lifeboats, there was a hail from the destroyer's bridge.

'Lifeboats ahoy!' The voice, as it went on, was slow and deliberate and Kuroda frowned impatiently at the implication that he spoke no English. In fact he spoke the language well, as did many Japanese officers. 'You will come alongside, starboard side aft. I shall embark all hands. If you give trouble I shall open fire. I hope that is clearly understood.' There was a pause. 'You British troops. I rely on you to make sure the Japs understand what I've said.'

Kuroda was impelled to speak out. In a high, harsh voice he called back, 'I understand. I am Commander Kuroda, of the Imperial Japanese Navy. I speak excellent English.'

'Good,' Cameron answered. 'I'm asking for your word that you won't give any trouble.'

There was no answer from Kuroda; not in English, not to Cameron. There was what sounded like a command in his own language and the men along the destroyer's decks saw the glint of steel as rifles were lifted all along the line of boats. Petty Officer Jago yelled out a warning and as the Japanese rifles opened in a series of flashes the armed guard went flat, taking shelter where they could. Bullets whirred like bees, ricocheting off the upperworks, off the tubes and depth-charges. Jago gave no order to return the fire. Up to the skipper, he thought: *he* wasn't going to risk killing helpless pongoes. Bullets were now zipping around the bridge, and as Jago looked for'ard he saw the Oerlikon gunner on the starboard side just below the bridge fall back, away from his gun, and collapse in a heap below the break of the fo'c'sle. Then he saw something else: Cameron himself, taking the place of the gunnery rate and swinging the Oerlikon towards

106

the leading boat. There was a short burst of fire and the Jap who'd been doing the talking and giving the firing order took the result. His head seemed to disintegrate and the rest flopped overboard. Good shooting, Jago thought, spot-on, with none of the pongoes hit.

There was a lull in the firing, as though the Japs had been bludgeoned into having second thoughts. The lull continued; the firing was not in fact resumed. There was a curious silence; Jago, keeping his guard in cover, awaited orders from the bridge. Before they came he heard a distant sound, a throb of engines, coming closer.

ii

The radar had picked up the echo.

'Aircraft, sir, approaching, bearing green eight five, one in number.'

'Right!' It had to be a Jap. Cameron took up the loud-hailer and called down to the upper deck. 'Aircraft approaching starboard. All ack-ack guns' crews stand by.' He switched off and spoke to Pegram in the director. 'Fire as soon as it looks like attacking.'

'Aye, aye, sir!'

If it was a Jap, it would attack: there wasn't enough light from the moon and stars for anyone to be certain of seeing the markings. Cameron turned to Dawnay. 'Engines to full ahead, Pilot. Wheel amidships. I'll do the usual twist-and-turn act when the bugger's sighted.'

Dawnay passed the orders down to the wheelhouse. Cameron looked aft. The 3-inch HA gun mounting was already tracking round to cover the expected bearing, likewise the multiple pom-pom. There appeared to be nothing happening in the lifeboats, no more firing. Petty Officer Jago, obviously hoisting in the fact that there wouldn't be any embarkation yet awhile, had sent his armed seamen back to their action stations and was as it were distributing himself around the guns, chivvying the crews in a loud voice.

Aft again, the First Lieutenant had also sent his hands away to their stations and was moving for'ard towards the bridge, clasping his steel helmet hard down on his head.

The ominous sound of aircraft engines had increased. Cameron searched the sky, eyes aching with strain, staring ahead through his binoculars. It was the yeoman of signals who saw it first and yelled out.

'Dead ahead, sir! A big bastard . . . coming in for a bombing run now!'

Cameron gripped the rail ahead of his body, staring upwards. Then he, too, saw it, low and close. As his ack-ack went into action he saw the bomb doors open, saw the bombs drop like eggs, with residual forward speed on them, felt the wind of bullets as the rear-gunner opened fire. There was a scream of agony and behind him Dawnay fell to the deck aft of the binnacle. A spurt of blood reached Cameron and reddened his white uniform shirt. Then there was something like a cataclysm, a sustained roar of sound and a streaming mass of flame, red, orange, white. The *Caithness* shook right throughout her length, shook and drummed to more than her engines but so far as Cameron could tell hadn't been hit.

But something had been.

When the smoke had cleared away the sea was empty of lifeboats. There was just wreckage, some of it burning until the sea doused it, and a number of shattered bodies drifted idly in death, heads down in the water.

Then the aircraft came back in. This time it made its approach from astern, low as before, screaming over the destroyer's decks, apparently untouched by the ack-ack barrage. Once again the 3-inch HA fired rapid rounds amid an acrid stench of gun-smoke; the multiple pom-pom pumped away. Once again the bombs could be seen, coming for them at a flat angle. This time the Japanese aim was better: the stick took the water only some half a cable's-length from the port side of the racing, twisting destroyer, exploding on impact with the sea. A range of waterspouts arose, flinging spray over the decks and making the destroyer ring like a bell. The

First Lieutenant could be seen from the bridge, doubling along the upper deck with Petty Officer Bustacle and an engine-room rating from the damage-control party. He would be going below to check for leaks and sprung plates.

In the engine-room Mr Henty was hanging on tight to the guardrail of the starting platform as the hollow boom of the close explosions filled the engine spaces. It was just noise, he reckoned, they were okay so far. No trouble down here in the engine-room, anyway. Or nothing very much, just an injury . . . Stoker PO Tallis came through from the boiler room to make a report.

'All correct, sir. One man hurt, though. Slid on his arse, tore his bottom, twisted a leg at the same time, sir.'

'Bugger. Who, Tallis?'

Tallis said, 'Leading Stoker Zebedee.'

'That the moaner?'

Tallis gave a long-suffering nod. Zebedee had something worth moaning about now and would be taking full advantage of it, to Tallis' distraction till he was shifted off to the sick bay where he could moan at the quack and the SBA. As expected, the warrant engineer said Zebedee would have to lump it for the time being. He wasn't having any air locks opened up for cack-handed stokers to be carried to the quack, not while the attack was on. He said, 'Make him comfy if you can, Tallis.'

Tallis went back to the boiler-room, taking it carefully on the slippery, oily steel of the deck plating: the skipper was chucking the boat about all over the show, altering this way and that without cease. Tallis wished him all the luck in the world with his putting-off tactics. Not so Leading Stoker Zebedee. When Tallis returned, Zebedee stated his complaints.

' 'Snot right. In bloody agony I am! Skipper ought to 'ave some fucking consideration. Reckon me leg's broke.'

'Don't look like it to me,' Tallis said stonily. 'You can move the bloody article, I *see* you move it.' He raised his voice as Zebedee opened his mouth again. 'Skipper's got more to

worry about than you. So have we all. We'll all be bloody
lucky to come through this lot.'

'I – '

'Shut up, Zebedee.'

'You stupid bastard!'

Tallis went rigid. He bent as if to drag Zebedee up by the
scruff of the neck and then sock him one, a good smash in the
kisser. This impulse he resisted with difficulty: he was a PO and
wasn't going to lose his rate over Zebedee. But the past came
back to him – what had happened to his family, and now
Zebedee creating over a sore bum and a strained leg. He
didn't say anything, though. Any minute they might all be
dead and what Zebedee said or did would no longer matter.
He turned away as though he hadn't heard. He almost hadn't,
in fact; there was a terrible racket now, with the 3-inch
hammering away up topsides and the roar from the boilers
and the engines and now more explosions down the ship's
side.

iii

There were empty cartridge cases everywhere: Jago kicked
them over the side in heaps. The air was filled with the stench
of cordite; sweat poured from the ack-ack gunners. Ordinary
Seaman Roebuck had now replaced the dead starboard
Oerlikon gunner; Able Seaman Urridge, wishing desperately
he was back in his soft number in the wardroom pantry, had
been co-opted on to the 3-inch from his own action gun to
replace another casualty: Ordinary Seaman Burden. The Jap,
who so far hadn't been much use in regard to his bomb aimer,
had a good rear-gunner. The upper deck had been sprayed
like a rainstorm; the funnel was full of holes and there was
steam escaping from the uptakes, that and smoke. Burden
had been ripped apart, a line of bullets right up and down his
body. Not just Burden: six others, including Shiner White,
who had put his head out of the wheelhouse door at an
inopportune moment and would go no more a-whoring in

Trincomalee or any other of the world's ports and whose collection of dirty postcards would now be sold in a messdeck auction for the financial benefit of his widow. Jago, bracing himself for the next bombing and machine-gunning run, wondered if he was about to buy it too. He'd already taken some near misses: there were two bullet holes in his short-sleeved shirt and he'd lost his tin hat, bounced over the side by a shot that would have blown his brains out if the tin hat hadn't been there. Sardonically, Jago reckoned that there was one bloke aboard who wasn't going to get hit by any bullets and that was Jimmy the One. Jago had seen the First Lieutenant beating it below after opening up the clips on the door into the galley flat and the messdecks. Damage control, of course. Damage control my arse, Jago thought. It was a case of sod you, Jack, I'm making sure I'm all right. He wondered if the skipper was having similar thoughts. If he had time to have any at all: Jago reckoned he was handling the ship beautifully and never giving the Jap a chance to line things up properly and bring his sights right on.

And now the next attack was coming in.

This time, from ahead again. Everything was firing from the *Caithness*, a stream of shells and bullets, tracer arcing up for the Jap's big belly, the 3-inch looking as though it was on fire itself, flash after flash after flash and the breech opening and shutting again to the thrust of Urridge's clenched fist on the arse end of the projies.

Bombs away again. Jago watched them in a kind of awed fascination. Never mind the skipper's off-throwing antics, it was incredible to Jago that anyone, even a bleeding Jap, could be such a piss-poor bomb aimer, not that he himself had any personal experience of bombs other than at the receiving end. Or, in this current case, the spectator end. For that was what it was: like the preceding attacks, the bombs went straight into the hogwash. Jago was about to hoot derision up into the air, almost as though giving a bollocking for wetness to one of his own guns' crews, when the Jap bought it. A stream of tracer went up from the starboard Oerlikon, straight as a die into the cockpit, shattering the Perspex. Jago was convinced that, in the split-second the cockpit was in his view, he saw the spatter of the pilot's blood in the light of the moon. The aircraft seemed to waggle, to stagger and then, around two cables'-lengths astern of the *Caithness*, it dipped suddenly and plunged nose down into the water where it went under, rose again, and then began to settle.

Jago found Urridge beside him. 'Who did that for God's sake?' Urridge asked.

Jago said in astonishment, 'Starboard Oerlikon . . . bloody Roebuck! Your mate, bloody Roebuck!' He stared aft towards the sinking aircraft, now drawing away to starboard as Cameron altered course to circle back and look for survivors. Now there would be a lull. But only a lull, in Jago's view. The Jap would have made radio contact with his base, of course, indicating that he was attacking a British destroyer.

From now on they would be a target to be stalked and killed.

10

SOME FORTY SEA MILES ahead of the *Caithness* the dawn was coming up out of the east, brilliant and many-coloured, spreading over the ships of the Japanese convoy. Following upon the American attack, so fortunately for the Japanese broken off at an early stage, only two small escort vessels were left to guard the remaining merchant ships. Two had been sunk, a troop transport and a smaller vessel carrying stores for the army in Burma. A third, another transport with British prisoners of war embarked, had been slightly damaged by a bomb that had exploded by her forefoot, right on the waterline. The bows were twisted out of shape and her speed had been reduced, but the fore collision bulkhead was holding and the ship was thought to be seaworthy. The remainder of the convoy consisted of an armament carrier and a tanker, valuable prizes left unscathed by the US aircraft. Aboard the troop transport, the *Yokosuka Maru*, some of the lifeboats had been swung out as a precaution, enough to accommodate the Japanese crew and guards. If there was an emergency there would be no time to get the British prisoners up from below, thus it was considered pointless to swing out more boats.

Neither the vivid colours of the dawn nor the fresh air of the early morning, the welcome freshness that came before the day's heat struck, penetrated the battened-down troop-decks where some two thousand British soldiers, officers and men from a number of different corps and units, were huddled in stinking conditions and total discomfort under the constantly watchful Japanese guards carrying sub-machine-guns which no one doubted would be used in wholesale slaughter just as soon as one of the Japs grew trigger-happy.

'Just waiting for an excuse,' an infantryman said. His face was covered with suppurating sores and his limbs shook as though he had the plague. 'Let's hope no sod gives it to 'em!'

'Quickest way out. . . .'

'Speak for yourself, mate. Me, I want to get through this war.'

The other man was little more than a skeleton, a khaki-drill bag of brittle bones that ached with weariness and semi-starvation. No more than twenty, he looked an old man. Even his hair was thinning, falling out. They were all lethargic now, most were sick from one cause or another, and all without real hope that they would ever come through. The rumour had run that the Jap bastards had a railway line to lay and they, the prisoners of war, were going to be the slave labour, working their guts out fourteen hours or more a day, seven days a week, fifty-two weeks a year, in swamp and heat, covered with leeches, a prey to snakes and other unpleasantnesses, under the gun-butts and whips of the Jap guards. They would all work together, officers and men. To the Japs they were all the same, dishonoured creatures who had surrendered, no longer worthy in Japanese eyes to be rated as men.

'Ullage,' the infantryman said bitterly.

'Eh?'

'Ullage – that's us.'

There was no further response: the second man had sunk back into his own miseries. All around, they were the same. Listless, mere automatons that responded when necessary to Jap orders. There had been a thrill of excitement, a stir along the tight-packed troop-decks, when during the night the attack had come and they had heard the racket, the explosions, the dull booms that had gone through the transport and brought a surge of hope that their trap was to be

114

sprung, and, like lucky mice unexpectedly released, they might find salvation in the water. The drawing off of the attack had left them more hopeless than before.

After the attack they were given no news. Their transport steamed on, at a slower speed now. They had felt the thump from for'ard, and the deduction was easily enough made, but it brought no comfort. They were still bound for Rangoon or some other port in Burma, the Irrawaddy or some other river that would take them to the labour camps. If they were lucky they might be taken on in boats; if not, they would have to march. There was no escape. No escape from sheer torture, world without end, a half-life beneath the victorious Rising Sun. The Japs were invincible. Had been invincible from the start. No one who had served in Singapore in the pre-war days could believe, even now, that the British base could have folded so easily; no one could believe that the great new battleship *Prince of Wales* and the battle-cruiser *Repulse* had been sent to the bottom of the South China Sea, taking with them the flag of Rear-Admiral Tom Phillips, battered to his knees by Jap air attack. It was all incredible; and there had been Pearl Harbor, the ruthless, horrendous demise of the United States Pacific Fleet, battleships and cruisers shattered and pulverized at their berths. . . .

Suddenly a bombardier lurched to his feet, heaving himself up on the shoulders of those nearest. The moment he did so he was spotted by one of the guards.

A sub-machine-gun was raised and pointed, 'You sit down.'

'Look, I'm sick. I want to see the doctor.'

'No doctor for you. All are sick. You no sicker than others.'

The man swayed. 'I said I'm sick. I've a right to see a doctor.'

'No rights for prisoners. You are told to sit. You disobey. Come here.' The voice was a whiplash. Unsteady on his feet, the soldier obeyed. Reaching the guard, he awaited the punishment: four smashes across the cheeks, two one side, two the other, with the butt of a rifle wielded by another guard. Afterwards, his face was a bloodied mess and three teeth had been loosened. The soldiers along the troop-deck watched but no one interfered: there were too many guns. When an officer wearing the crown and star of a lieutenant-colonel and the badges of a crack infantry regiment made a formal protest, he was called out and given the same punishment.

The transport steamed on, and the sun came fully over the horizon to start the torture of its heat.

ii

'I don't understand it,' Cameron said. 'I'd have expected a follow-up.' He was speaking to the First Lieutenant, who had reported the ship sound and seaworthy, unscathed except for the cannon fire from the aircraft: that, and the casualties already accorded their sea burials.

Main said, 'Maybe they're concentrating on convoy protection. They'll be assuming that's where we're bound, I expect.'

'Two birds with one stone, Number One?'

'Something like that, sir.'

'Well, you could be right.' Cameron glanced at his watch and did a quick calculation. He was already missing his navigating officer; Dawnay had always had the answers ready, everything worked out in anticipation of what Cameron would want. 'We'll know before long. It's not far off first light. We should be raising the convoy any time now.' He turned as the doctor appeared at the head of the starboard ladder. 'Well, doc. How are things in your sphere?'

'Walking wounded . . . none of them bad. Flesh wounds – they'll be all right.'

'Thank God for that.' One of the casualties was Petty Officer Bustacle, who'd taken a bullet across his rump and wouldn't sit down for a while. Cameron would be happier when he knew his chief bosun's mate was fully fit again; he asked about him.

116

'Bustacle? Nothing to worry about there. Just a bit sore, that's all.' Yeoman of Signals Venner heard that, and wished all he had to worry about himself was a glanced-off Jap bullet. He was still wondering whether or not to go to the quack as soon as they were fallen out from action stations, though God knew when that would be now, or give the Germolene a bit longer to act. Or he might compromise: go along and see the piss-pot jerker in the sick bay and get some unofficial advice about his bottom. It was likely enough the SBA knew more about those sort of diseases than the quack himself. RNVR quacks hadn't the experience, not when they hadn't been in long anyway. After a while, of course, they became as expert as the RN medics who spent their whole careers just treating VD. . . .

Styles was about to say something further when the sound-powered telephone whined and Cameron took it up. 'Bridge, Captain here – '

'PO Tel, sir. Cypher coming through, sir, from Trinco.'

'Right, thank you, Potts. As soon as you have it, send it along to the doctor.' Cameron put down the telephone and turned to Styles. 'Work, doc. A cypher . . . deal with it as fast as you can, all right?'

Styles nodded. 'Orders, d'you suppose?'

'Or information. We'll have to wait and see.'

'Let's hope C-in-C's sending assistance,' Main said. Cameron glanced at him. The First Lieutenant's face seemed to be showing the strain, either of the war or of keeping his end up in front of the ship's company. As Main left the bridge Cameron gave a sigh; he'd had the lower deck's attitude very much in mind but had found no way of easing the situation for his First Lieutenant other than to treat him precisely as he had always done, so that full accord showed between the two senior officers. You couldn't get on the Tannoy and say to the ship's company, in so many words, that the First Lieutenant wasn't a scrimshanker but had emerged from danger as his bounden duty – especially when you weren't entirely convinced yourself. Cameron's long-term hope was that once his report went in for consideration by Captain(D), Main would be withdrawn from the ship; but in the meantime the situation had to be coped with as best possible. It wasn't the happiest atmosphere in which to be steaming into further action.

iii

Petty Officer Jago had been round the gun positions for the hundredth time. In consultation with Lieutenant Pegram it had been decided to shift Ordinary Seaman Roebuck permanently, or at any rate for the remainder of the patrol, to the position of starboard Oerlikon gunner. Roebuck had done well, if only by the sheerest luck, and the destruction of the Jap aircraft had done a lot for morale throughout the ship. As Stripey Gizzard remarked to Leading Seaman Prosser, if a half-hard little bolshie git of an OD, and hostilities only at that, could shoot down a bloody great Jap all on his tod, well, there must be life in the British Navy yet.

Jago stopped by the Oerlikon, where Roebuck was in the straps and swinging the gun like a professional, aiming at imaginary enemies.

Jago said, 'Don't let it go to your head, son.'

'What, GI?'

'The thin red line of heroes stuff.'

'Just a fluke, GI,' Roebuck said modestly, but it was clear he didn't really regard it as that.

'Not 'arf,' Jago said sardonically. 'Just the same – you did all right and I'm proud of you. Keep it up.'

Roebuck was speechless: praise from the GI was as rare as milk from a bull. He watched Jago making his way aft to Three and Four guns, halting en route at the 3-inch HA. Roebuck saw him nattering away at Urridge and the rest of the gun's crew and gesturing back towards the Oerlikon. Roebuck got the idea he was being held up as a shining example, the young but dependable gunnery rate, pride of the Indian Ocean and the Eastern Fleet. It wasn't every Jolly Jack who could claim his own personal aircraft. He might even get a gong out of it – a mention in despatches at the very least, like the pongoes got when they'd done something special. Life aboard looked like being very much better from now on: he'd never been appreciated before, anyway not since leaving the Landport Drapery Bazaar. When he got back to Pompey he'd have news to make the whole accounts department sit up. . . .

Roebuck swung himself round and round in the leather harness of the Oerlikon and started uttering *phut-phut-phut* sounds, rather loudly. When the skipper got on the Tannoy and announced that two hands at a time from each gun could take a chance to nip below to go to the heads, but stand by for the action alarm while doing so, Roebuck was approached by Able Seaman Urridge.

'Dog with two tails if not more,' Urridge said with a sniff.

'So what?'

'Don't you so-what me, sonny boy.'

'Sorry.'

Urridge came closer and lowered his voice. 'Don't forget, we 'ave a pact like: watch Jimmy.'

'I won't forget,' Roebuck said.

'Better not.' Urridge turned away and went back to his gun. Roebuck looked after him, frowning. He was suddenly seeing Urridge differently. Urridge was an ungainly figure, shambling and not over-clean, and his face was always as sour as junket, as though he had a perpetual liver. Out for himself, was Urridge. Drop anybody in it if he saw a personal advantage, probably. . . . Roebuck had gone along with him largely because they were two loners, out of the normal camaraderie of the messdeck. In two words, not popular. Of course, Roebuck wouldn't back-track on Jimmy's reprehensible act of buggering off from a tight spot – he wouldn't back-track on trying to ensure that even a bloody Officer got what he deserved – but there was an undeniable difference now Roebuck had proved himself in the eyes of the lads, even to the undreamed-of extent of getting a word of praise out of

119

the GI. All of a sudden some advice from the past came back as clear as day to Ordinary Seaman Roebuck: the words of old Mr Lampeter, chief wages clerk at the LDB, who'd always kept a fatherly – almost a grandfatherly – eye on him in the long ago as it all now seemed. Mr Lampeter, who had a face like parchment and wheezed constantly with asthma, had commented on his friendship with another clerk who was later given the sack for general uselessness and a disregard for the truth. He'd said in his sepulchral, rather ominous way, 'Watch who you make friends of, Roebuck. Watch carefully.'

'How d'you mean, Mr Lampeter?' Roebuck had asked, all innocence.

Mr Lampeter had prodded him in the ribs with a fountain pen. 'You know very well what I mean, Roebuck. You've a good position here as a clerk. You could have prospects.' Prospects had always been important to Mr Lampeter, who expected in time, if he lived much longer that was, to advance his own prospects to six quid a week. 'Don't – er – dirty your own doorstep.'

'But I – '

'Mark my words, young man. There's always people who'll drag someone down with them, given half a chance. You know the saying, I'm sure.'

'What saying, Mr Lampeter?'

Mr Lampeter had looked into his face very solemnly indeed. 'Birds of a feather, Roebuck, flock together. My advice is, don't risk getting tarred with a doubtful brush.'

Two sayings for the price of one. At the time Roebuck had jeered in private, but now, at long last, he was beginning to see the point. Undoubtedly Urridge was poorly feathered and could be said to be a very doubtful brush in the eyes of the officers. And tar, of course, stuck. Roebuck began *phutphutting* again. Two aircraft, or even more, would be that much better than one.

But perhaps that was pushing it a little far.

120

Styles brought the cypher to the bridge and handed the transcript to Cameron. 'Short but sweet enough,' he said.

Cameron read. Help on the way: a squadron of torpedo-bombers, Barracudas, was being flown off into the area of the position reported by the US strike force and would be in the vicinity within the next two hours together with a fighter escort of Fulmars.

'No particular orders for us,' Styles remarked.

'No, but they're implicit, doc. We're not being ordered to lay off and that's good enough for me.' He caught sight of Main, coming for'ard from the tubes, and called to him. Main quickened his pace and climbed to the bridge. Cameron handed him the PL version of the cypher.

Main said, 'Barracudas and Fulmars. Probably from a carrier.'

'Yes. A carrier that'll be under orders to keep out of the area herself I shouldn't wonder.' Aircraft-carriers were seldom put at unnecessary risk themselves; they were too big, too vulnerable, too expensive to lose or refit. Aircraft themselves were relatively expendable and there was a feeling in the air that that was how C-in-C was regarding the *Caithness* – expendable. There was no suggestion of any surface support, but that could well be simply because, as Cameron had realized earlier, there was nothing within immediate steaming distance of the *Caithness* or the Jap convoy.

Meantime they should be sighting the convoy at any moment. Cameron once again used the Tannoy to address his ship's company. He said, 'Assistance is on its way. There's not long to go now. All hands stood down are to return to their action stations immediately.'

He switched off. He had scarcely done so when there was a shout from the yeoman of signals. 'Smoke, sir, bearing green two oh. I reckon it's the convoy.'

Cameron nodded and lifted his glasses on the bearing. He saw the smudges of smoke, the ships themselves still hull down beyond the horizon of a brightening dawn. He said, 'Right, Yeoman! Bend on the battle ensign.' He brought his binoculars down again and called to Pegram in the director. In director firing, all the destroyer's guns moved to line up on the enemy.

11

Under full power the *Caithness* rushed on across the sea still empurpled by the early morning, her wake streaming white and tumbling astern, a wide swathe across the brilliance. In that calm sea she seemed to hurtle like an express train, her plates vibrant to the thrust of the engines and the White Ensign streaming bar taut in the wind made by the vessel's own passage. By now the radar had reported the echoes and from the forebridge Cameron had the Japanese ships in sight: two small escorts and three merchantmen, one of them seemingly down by the bows.

Lieutenant Ringrose, action oow in place of Dawnay, was looking out ahead. He said, 'Doesn't seem as if they've spotted us, sir.'

'Any moment now,' Cameron said, also watching closely. The distant escorts looked placid and unsuspicious, certainly, moving along their set course northwards and not turning to intercept, to put themselves between the attack and the convoy. The convoy was moving slowly, something of a sitting duck, presumably on account of the evident damage to the bows of one of the merchant ships, a big one that Cameron believed to have been a peacetime liner and now almost certainly acting as a troop transport. Then, as he watched out, there was a puff of smoke and a flash from the fore part of the transport, followed almost immediately by another from a gun mounted aft.

'Stand by,' Cameron said. 'Six-inch projies on the way over. Yeoman – '

'Sir?'

'Hoist the battle ensign.' Cameron called up the director. 'I'll open as soon as we're inside the range.' Then he called Mr Henty in the engine-room, telling him what was happening.

Seconds later Mr Henty felt the concussions for himself as they echoed and rang through the engine-room plates. Near misses, he reckoned, very near misses and very good shooting indeed for a first ranging salvo. But at least it wasn't a hit – yet. Grim-faced the warrant engineer watched the telegraphs from the bridge. Any moment now the skipper would be doing all he could to throw off the Jap range-takers and layers by twisting and turning and altering his speed, the same old game that had been played intermittently throughout what was becoming a bloody long war.

ii

Up there in the director Pegram had a good bird's eye view of the bridge and the whole of the upper deck from stem to stern. He glanced along it as he waited for the Captain's order to open fire. Aft by the torpedo-tubes he saw Mr Clinch, all ready with his torpedo party and staring towards the enemy, a hand lifted to shield his eyes from the blinding sun. It wasn't the best approach for an attack by guns or torpedoes, right into that sun, but they had no option about that. Petty Officer Jago was well in evidence, arms a-swing, back straight as the ramrod he liked to be, tin hat square on his head and his voice raucous as he spread his own particular brand of cheer and encouragement. The First Lieutenant was checking around the fo'c'sle, just about finishing now and moving past the hurricane-twisted barrel and shield of One gun. Pegram fancied there was a touch of haste in Main's movements, as though he wanted to put more than fresh air between himself and any gunfire, but possibly that was uncharitable: as damage-control officer, Main would have plenty to check and later plenty to do if they got hit.

Meanwhile the Japs seemed to be in no hurry to follow up that first nicely-placed salvo and by this time they'd lost the advantage since the destroyer was no longer where it was when they'd opened. Cameron was flinging her about all over the place. Pegram thought about the Jap gunners: merchant ships didn't make good gun platforms and you couldn't open from them with too many guns at once or you would start the plates. Pegram had heard stories about even the battleships *Nelson* and *Rodney*, each with their nine 16-inch guns in turrets along the fore deck: when they'd opened for a practice shoot, all nine together, shortly after being commissioned for the first time, they'd split the fo'c'sle, opening up the deck like a sardine can. Thereafter neither of them had been able to fire off a full broadside. And they were battleships, built for the firing of their guns. As for the Japs . . . maybe the opposition was not going to be as tough as he'd feared. Also, the 6-inches aboard the transport were almost certainly old and could be liable to misfires and a general buggering up of the electrics and other mechanisms.

Lucky for the *Caithness* . . .

In Pegram's mind there were positive signs that God was on their side and he was still convinced they would come through: they were there in the cause of saving souls as much as killing them. The actual sight of that transport with its supposed cargo of British prisoners of war had brought the destroyer's current mission much more sharply into focus, Pegram had found. Nothing would be spared in the attempt to free the troops and take them aboard if the transport had to be sunk, or to escort them across the Bay of Bengal to Trincomalee under the umbrella of British air cover when it materialized. Pegram looked at his watch: too soon to expect them yet.

Then the guns opened again. This time the fall of shot wasn't so good. Cameron's antics were paying off. Soon after this, the orders came from the bridge: they were within range.

125

'Target, the leading escort. All guns open fire.'

Pegram acknowledged, led the guns on to the indicated target, and pressed his firing button. The electrical impulses went direct to the guns and there was a concerted crash that took some of the way off the ship, jerking her in the water, and clouds of smoke billowed to bring with them the stench of cordite. As the guns' crews along the decks reloaded and reported ready, Pegram watched the fall of shot.

Not too bad.

The escort had disappeared behind spouts of ocean but only temporarily: a moment later she emerged, steaming still and moving fast, turning under full port wheel towards the destroyer to present a smaller target. And the transport was in action again: the smoke, the flash and then seconds later the whine of a shell passing overhead, uncomfortably close to the director. Pegram ducked his head instinctively, banged his chin on his instruments, and swore vividly; then the orders came up from the bridge to open in rapid firing. As more shells came across from the troop transport, the destroyer closed fast towards the leading escort, all her guns pumping out shells, still concentrating on the one Japanese ship.

Watching closely, Cameron saw the result of good firing: the escort vessel, steaming through the fall of shot as before, showed a lick of flame, fire coming up through her super-structure and a curious glow from below. Then, with a heavy explosion that came back towards the destroyer, and a sheet of flame, she blew up.

Cameron said, 'Cease firing. Shift target – the second escort.' From along his decks he heard the cheering as the sweating, dirt-streaked gunners in their white anti-flash gear paused for a moment to await the order to open again. Cameron took up the Tannoy. 'Well done all hands,' he said. 'Keep it up. I'm now going for the other escort.' Putting down the Tannoy, he passed the word to the director to resume rapid firing.

Pegram had already laid and trained on the remaining escort. Once again as the gun-ready lamps came on he pressed his firing button. Once again the *Caithness* shook and rattled to the discharge of the guns. By the tubes Mr Clinch walked up and down, outwardly calm at what was a nail-biting moment: he wanted a share of the action but wasn't going to get it by the look of things. The guns would deal with that second Jap bastard, he reflected, as easily as they had done the first. And the skipper, for obvious reasons, wouldn't be mounting any attack on the transport, not until he knew for sure whether or not there were British prisoners aboard. Of course, that left the other two ships of the convoy . . . maybe something would come his way yet. He reckoned the skipper would go in and sink the tanker and the other ship; they both carried guns aft, Mr Clinch could see, and they were in action along with the troop transport. He turned and glanced for'ard towards the bridge as if trying to assess what Cameron might be going to do, and he was looking that way when a projectile took the director and disintegrated it.

iii

The ship was turning under full port wheel when the director went. It continued to do so: no orders reached Chief PO Chapman in the wheelhouse. Cameron, caught by the blast, lay huddled in a corner of the bridge. Ringrose was dead, lying in a pool of blood, taken right through the neck by a steel sliver driven down from the director's wreckage. Venner, yeoman of signals with now unnecessary fears about his bottom, had vanished, blown clear off the flag deck and over the side, dead in fact before he hit the water. The ordinary seaman acting as starboard lookout was moaning on a high monotonous note, eyes staring at nothing. One man was miraculously unhurt: another OD, the port lookout. Blood, Pegram's blood with it, dripped down the remains of the tripod mast that had supported the director just abaft the bridge.

Below in the wheelhouse the Coxswain called the bridge; no

127

response. 'You,' he said to the telegraphsman. 'Nip up and take a look. Report down the voice-pipe, all right?'

'Yes, 'Swain – '

'At the double, then, lad.' Chapman wiped pouring sweat from his face: he kept the wheel on full, you always obeyed the last order. The *Caithness* continued to circle, continued too to fire her guns, now in quarters firing. Jago had seen to that. When the director had gone and he couldn't see anyone on the bridge, he hadn't wasted any time in waiting for orders that wouldn't ever come if all the bridge personnel had bought it along with Mr Pegram and the director's crew. He took charge himself, all the guns at once so far as possible, an almost maniacal figure in white shirt and shorts that were virtually all-over black by now, what with the smoke and all.

From the bridge the telegraphsman reported down to the coxswain. 'No one left, 'Swain – '

'The Captain?'

'I – I think he's dead.'

Chapman swore, softly to himself. Then he eased the wheel: no point in going round and round like a maypole. Up the pipe he called, 'Get the doctor up there, for God's sake! And the First Lieutenant.'

'Aye, aye, 'Swain.' There was a pause, then, 'Officer coming up now, 'Swain.'

'Who?'

'Mr Tillotson.'

'The middy? John the Baptist on a motor-bike!'

'What was that, 'Swain?'

'Never bloody mind, lad. Put Mr Tillotson on the voice-pipe.' He waited, then heard a thin nervous voice trying to announce itself. He said, 'That you, Mr Tillotson?'

'Yes, it is, Cox'n.'

'Waiting for orders, sir.'

'We'd better wait for the First Lieutenant, . . '

'I don't think we had, sir. We haven't got all flipping day. How's the Captain?'

'I – I don't know.'

128

Then bloody well find out, was what Chapman wanted to say, but didn't. That Tillotson was very young all said and done, only just off mother's milk. He needed a sea-daddy as the saying went. Chapman did his best to fill the role and keep the midshipman on an even keel until Jimmy the One turned up – and where, for God's sake, was *he*? Chapman said, speaking slowly and with emphasis, 'Now listen, sir. The Captain, he'd want to steer towards the Japs, right? So if you'll give the order, sir, put me on course to close, well, that'll make everything all official like, won't it, eh?'

'Yes.' Tillotson's voice was firmer, he seemed to be taking a grip. 'All right, Cox'n. Steer oh eight five degrees.'

'Steer oh eight five, sir,' Chapman repeated in relief. Poor little bugger, probably peeing his pants like all-get-out. The *Caithness* moved on, still under full power, flinging herself towards the enemy. Chapman called up the voice-pipe again. 'Bridge, sir? Best inform the engine-room what's happened. They like to be kept in touch with events, see.'

'Yes, Cox'n.' Midshipman Tillotson was about to call Mr Henty when the doctor appeared at the head of the ladder, carrying his action bag of tricks. Tillotson gestured at the huddled figure of the Captain in the corner by the fore screen, and Styles went across and bent down by him. After half a minute he straightened.

'It's all right, Mid. He'll live. Concussed, that's all. I'll just make him comfortable.' Styles shifted Cameron's limbs, straightening him out, looking around for something to lay his head on, and chose the flag locker as a fruitful source. He pulled out a number of flags and pennants, rolled them into something like a pillow, and shoved the bunch behind Cameron's head. That done, there wasn't much to see to: the port lookout had stopped his high moaning and lay still, eyes staring, this time with the glaze of death.

Tillotson said, 'The Captain. Wouldn't he be better below?'

'Yes. But he's already starting to come round. He wouldn't

thank me for making him climb to the bridge again. You know the Captain, Mid. Place of duty and all that!'

Tillotson gave a nervous grin. The doctor was right.

iv

Cameron came round just in time to hear more cheering from the upper deck. The First Lieutenant, now on the bridge, was bending over him. He shook his head, felt immediate pain, and kept still. It hurt even to open his eyes. In a weak voice he asked 'What happened?'

Main told him, and added, 'That cheering – if you heard it, sir. We've got the second escort. There's just the convoy now.'

'We're not firing. . . .'

'I ordered the cease fire.'

'Why?'

Main said, 'That liner, the troop transport as it may be. You won't want to open fire on her.'

'No, I won't.' Cameron opened his eyes again, tried to pull himself upright, but slumped back again to await more strength in his limbs. 'But there's the others, Number One. They've got guns too . . . they'll have to be silenced.'

'I needed your orders,' Main said with a touch of huffiness.

When the Captain was out like a light, the First Lieutenant usually took over automatically; but Cameron didn't argue the point. That could come later. All he said was, 'Resume the action, Number One. Quarters firing . . . poor Pegram. He was so sure he was coming through. It's up to Jago now. Or Mr Clinch.'

'Clinch? We'd have to close to within torpedo range, sir.'

'Yes, Number One, we would.'

'Easy target for the Jap guns.'

'It's what we're here for. Anyway, we still have the gunpower, Number One. I won't be using the torpedoes until I have to. Pass the word, resume firing. Target, the tanker and the store ship if that's what she is. Leave the transport.'

130

'Aye, aye, sir,' Main said, and turned away down the ladder. Cameron heaved himself up again, felt a shade better. Styles was still on the bridge; he helped Cameron to his feet and guided him across to the Captain's high stool. Cameron got his bottom on it and rested his forearms on the shelf below the fore screen.

'All right?' Styles asked.

'Yes, thank you.'

'You're sure?'

'Yes. I'll be all right. Better get back to the sick bay, doc. There's others who'll be needing you more.'

Styles shook his head. 'Not true, sir. The earlier wounded are fine. And this last lot . . . we didn't get any wounded by some miracle. Only dead.'

'Only dead,' Cameron repeated, and put his head down on his arms. There was a feeling of giddiness, as though he were about to pass out again, but it left him quite quickly. Only dead . . . and his own responsibility because he had taken the ship out of his routine patrol, strictly in disobedience of orders. But something had had to be done for those prisoners of war . . . he made an effort and turned his body on the stool to give a grin of encouragement to Midshipman Tillotson. Tillotson who didn't like the sea, Tillotson who had made a wrong choice of career and was now stuck fast in the war at sea and could be steaming now towards his own armageddon: Cameron expected aerial attack at any moment and his only wonder was that the Jap planes hadn't come in already.

He said, 'Scared, Mid?'

Tillotson returned the grin, nervously and uncertainly. Cameron said, 'Don't bother to answer that. I know you're scared. So am I. So's everyone aboard, unless they're crazy. Or have no imagination. So don't let that worry you.'

'No, sir.'

'I'll be relying on you as my action oow. There's not many of us left now. The hands'll be relying on us all and we can't let them down.'

'No, sir. I'll be all right, sir.'

Cameron nodded: a twinge of pain passed through his head. He said, 'Yes, I know you will.' He hoped he had made a point that would penetrate: the point that so many men in action were afraid not so much of what might happen as of the simple fact of showing fear before the others. Once a youngster hoisted in that he was not alone in that, he was part of the way towards containing his fears. No one ever really believed anything was going to happen to himself and if the other fear could be staved off . . . but then Pegram had been convinced that he bore a charmed life and everyone aboard knew it. The fact that he'd gone was going to be a blow at faith. Not that there was anything to be done about that.

The guns were in action again now and the gap between the destroyer and the three merchant ships had narrowed far enough. Cameron ordered a turn to port to bring his ship broadside to the convoy, or what was left of it, and so give himself the full advantage of all his guns. Until the Jap aircraft came in, there could be no doubt of the result of the action: though the merchant ships were firing still their aim was poor, and the shells from the *Caithness* were having their due effect. As Cameron watched, the after 6-inch aboard the store ship took what looked like a direct hit and vanished in a red and orange explosion that sent the debris of metal and bodies flinging high into the air. Then the tanker was struck by a projectile that must have gone right into one of her cargo tanks. There was an almighty flash and an explosion, and flames roared high, seeming to spread almost at once along the whole length of her decks, enveloping the bridge and all the midship superstructure, and the poop. Figures could be seen running like lunatics along the flying bridges, emerging from the smoke and flames at either end, their clothing alight, some of them jumping into the water in a doomed attempt to avoid being burned alive, only to drop into oil-covered sea with the flames racing out from the tanker's riven hull to overwhelm them and crisp them into husks.

Tillotson was looking as though he were about to bring his stomach up, his face grey and working with sheer horror. In a high voice he asked, 'Are you going in for survivors, sir?'

Cameron brought his glasses down with a jerk. 'No, Mid. Look for yourself. None of them have a hope in hell of lasting more than seconds. And we have a job yet to do: those soldiers. Keep your thoughts on them.'

v

Along the upper deck they could feel the heat from the blazing tanker, coming across like the fires of hell itself. Ordinary Seaman Roebuck felt it as he lay back in the harness of his Oerlikon, waiting for the Jap aircraft to appear, as surprised as Cameron that they hadn't yet shown. In that heat he could almost smell the sharp stench of burning flesh, or maybe that was just imagination. But that could happen to him when the Japs came in . . . he felt fear rip at his guts, making him physically weak. Now, with the convoy almost all gone, was surely the time to piss off out of it and get beneath the nice, safe umbrella of the carrier-borne squadron coming to their assistance with the fighter escort that would engage the Japs. Roebuck reckoned it was lunacy, to try to shepherd that transport in, right across the hogwash to Trincomalee . . . he saw Petty Officer Jago looking up at him from the midship superstructure as a lull came in the firing.

Jago asked, 'Well, Roebuck, all ready for a repeat performance, are you?'

'I think it's daft,' Roebuck said. He found that his hands were shaking so badly that he could scarcely get a proper grip of the Oerlikon.

'What's daft, eh?'

'We haven't a hope. Once the Japs come in – '

'You'll shoot the buggers down, Roebuck. Won't you? My star performer on the close-range weapons, eh? You won't let me down, will you?'

Roebuck said, 'I dunno.'

The GI's face was suddenly like a rock. He said, '*You* don't know. I *do*. You'll do it again now you've done it once. If you don't – '

'It was a bloody fluke! That's all it was. You can't blame me if I don't get another, GI.'

'No. I wouldn't attempt to, lad.' Jago was studying him, eyes narrowed. Jago hadn't liked the sound of his voice, had recognized incipient panic. 'No one can do better than his best. Just see that you do that, that's all. I'll be watching you.' The GI turned about, straight-backed as ever, arms starting their Whale Island swing. Suddenly something seemed to burst in Roebuck's head: the GI was getting at him, getting ready to run him in, up on the bridge on a charge of cowardice in face of the enemy, or something, preparing the ground in advance. He screamed out, his voice clear along the deck as the lull in the firing continued. 'It's not bloody fair! It's not bloody right! Bloody officers can get away with it, like bloody Jimmy!'

The GI halted, stood stock still, his face ugly now. He turned about again and marched back to stand below the Oerlikon. He said stonily, 'That's a mutinous statement, Ordinary Seaman Roebuck, and duly noted as such. When the ship pulls out of action, you'll be taken under escort before the officer of the watch.'

He turned and marched away again. Roebuck stared after him, his face working, his whole body shaking now. He pushed up with his feet, depressing the angle of fire of the Oerlikon as he trained the gun round towards the GI. Sweat broke out when he realized the direction of his own thoughts. He swung back again – before anyone had noticed, he hoped. Sanity returned. It wouldn't do any good anyway, to knock off the GI, say in the middle of action when it next came – even if he got away with it, he knew his voice had been heard by everyone on the upper deck. Urridge wasn't meeting his eye; Urridge, when the crunch came, wouldn't want to know. Urridge looked after himself, got others to do his dirty work. No charges of mutiny or insubordination for Able Seaman Urridge, oh no.

On the bridge, Cameron had heard the shouting and recognized the beginnings of hysteria. He had also seen the way Roebuck had swivelled the Oerlikon. He acted fast: he spoke down the voice-pipe to the coxswain. 'Did you hear that, Chapman?'

'I did, sir.'

'I don't suppose there's anyone who didn't. See that Roebuck's taken off the Oerlikon – inform the GI and tell him I want to see him ón the bridge immediately. Fast as you can make it, Cox'n.'

'Aye, aye, sir.' Chapman wiped the back of a hand across his face and sent the wheelhouse messenger for the gunner's mate. There was going to be much trouble, Chapman knew, and it couldn't have come at a worse moment. No mention from the skipper yet of charges, but that would have to come. You couldn't let an OD get away with shouting his mouth off in the way Roebuck had. On the bridge Cameron was livid – with Roebuck, with Main, with the GI and with himself, though he still didn't see how he could have handled the affair of Main any differently. Basically, it came down to Main himself. By his action in the tiller flat, Main had brought this about. . . .

Petty Officer Jago came up the ladder. 'Wanted to see me, sir.'

'Yes, GI. What was all that about?'

'You heard what was said, did you, sir?'

'Yes, of course I did. I want to know what precipitated it.' Cameron added, 'This is between you and me, GI. It may be unorthodox, but we happen to be in action. You understand?'

'Yessir, I understand.'

'I saw Roebuck swing his Oerlikon towards you, GI. That's why I'm taking him off the gun. It's also why I want the facts, here and now. What's the connection?'

Jago bit his lip, seeing the way the thing was going. But he came out with it straight. 'Could be my fault, sir. I tried to put a touch of stiffening in Roebuck. He didn't like it. I'm glad you've took him off the gun, sir.'

'It didn't go beyond stiffening?'

Jago shook his head. 'No, sir, it did not. You have my word, sir.'

'All right, GI. that's good enough for me. Put Roebuck where he can't do any harm while we're in action – I'll leave that to you. Now tell me something else; what's being said on the lower deck about the First Lieutenant?'

Jago hesitated, blew out his cheeks, looked away across the top of Cameron's head, and said, 'First Lieutenant, sir, didn't do himself much good in the tiller flat.'

Cameron nodded. 'All right, GI. Thank you.'

Jago saluted, turned smartly about and went back down the ladder to the guns. Cameron was left with his worries: his officer complement so much depleted, his First Lieutenant in effect a broken reed who from now on would command little respect. Roebuck's shouted words could prove a kind of cataclysm, producing a slow simmer that would spread right along the lower deck. Cameron felt out of his depth, without the long experience and training of the RN behind him. He was in irons as it were: there was really nothing he could do but watch the fuse burn down.

vi

'Turning,' Urridge said at the HA amidships. He spoke to Roebuck, shifted by the GI to act as a loading number, in effect a spare hand in a position where he could be watched and at the same time so could his mate Urridge. Petty Officer Jago had made no comment when he'd taken Roebuck off the Oerlikon, just given him the order, but Roebuck knew where the order had come from in the first place and was apprehensive about the future. He hadn't liked the look in the GI's face: in it he had read something like personal doom, and already Jago had uttered the word mutiny. . . .

'Turning,' Urridge said again. They came right round, a hundred and eighty degrees to starboard to bring the ship a little closer to the enemy as they made another firing run to rake the remaining store ship with their broadside. It was just a matter of time, Urridge said, standing and watching with nothing to do for the time being. He was right: just like the tanker, there was a sudden and immense explosion, slap amidships, and the store ship – which from the look of it was carrying ammunition – went up like a hundred bonfires, with debris scattering over a wide area, debris and bodies hurled into the air, arms and legs spread wide.

'That's about it,' Urridge said. 'I hope the skipper don't linger now. Get that trooper shifting west.'

Homeward bound, Roebuck thought. That was when his own personal trouble would come to a head. He was about to ask Urridge what he ought to do, what he ought to say to the skipper in order to steer clear of the worst charge any man could be faced with at sea, when they all heard the sounds, distant but approaching fast from the east, the Japanese air attack coming in at last.

12

THE REPORT from the radar was twelve aircraft. The 6-inch guns aboard the troop transport were firing still but with no effect. Cameron was moving too fast for the Jap gunners, twisting and turning to evade the bombers as they came in. This time they were dive bombers, screaming out of the sun, one after the other, bringing their own red Rising Suns down upon the *Caithness* at breakneck speed. The bombs fell, a whole series of near misses that rang like knells through the racing destroyer. The upper deck was drenched with spray from end to end. Below in the engine-room it was like being aboard a submarine under depth-charge attack. The same in the boiler-room where Stoker PO Tallis was doing his best to imagine he was back in Pompey barracks and about to go down Queen Street for a pint. It was a hard job but it was one way of keeping sane if you could manage it and at the same time keep an eye on your responsibilities. He was interrupted in his concentration by Leading Stoker Zebedee, back to duty from a short spell under the quack, who'd heaved him out as soon as he decently could, with his knee strapped.

Zebedee was moaning again: this time, a slightly burned hand.

'Look at it, PO.'

'I'm looking.'

'Well?'

138

'Kiss it better, shall I?'

Zebedee glared. 'That all you got to say, is it?'

'Yes,' Tallis answered. 'We're in bloody action, or didn't you guess?'

'Could go septic.'

'Could drop off. Just shut up, Zebedee.'

'That's all very well. If it was bloody Jimmy – '

'All right, all right, all right! That's enough about Jimmy. Remember you're a leading hand, Zebedee.' Stoker PO Tallis gave him a tap on the chest and stuck his lower lip out. 'I'm not having any yacking about Jimmy down here in my boiler-room – '

'The blokes in the seamen's mess – '

'Bollocks to 'em, Zebedee. You're not a bloke in the seamen's mess, I repeat, you're a leading hand, inflicted on me by God in an off moment to be number bleeding two in my watch. Just remember that if you want to keep your rate.'

'No need to threaten, PO.'

'I'm not threatening. I'm stating simple facts.' Tallis turned away, back to the boilers and the dials and gauges showing the head of steam. Much more fart-arsing around the hogwash at flat-out speeds and the oil fuel wouldn't hold up, which Tallis hoped the skipper would have in mind. They had a long haul home and they hadn't even started yet, and destroyers tended to drink it up when operating at maximum revolutions, just like his old dad had lapped up beer. His old dad had lapped up beer so fast and so often that he'd blown up, or more precisely had an ulcer that had burst and carried him off to his grave before his time. If he'd been cremated, Tallis reckoned he'd have put out the fires with the residue, smothered them like the ashes you shoved on to the furnaces in a coal burner to damp down and make smoke . . . and a few moments later Tallis was left wondering if he'd suffered some sort of premonition, because the word came through from the warrant engineer that the bridge was asking for smoke to be made. It was Chief ERA Trigg who brought the order, just as a very close near miss shuddered through the boiler-room causing Leading Stoker Zebedee to clutch for support with his burned hand. Zebedee yelled out loud, but no one was taking any notice, he might have been a lump of meat. Tallis passed the order for the fuel injection to be increased.

'Lively now, Zebedee!'

The thick black oil went into the furnaces, coursing from the jets in a heavy mist. Up top in the fresh air, the result was spewed from the funnel, as thick and black as the oil fuel itself, pouring aft like black treacle, overlaying the guns and the torpedo-tubes, overlaying Petty Officer Jago and Mr Clinch, who was still hoping for a torpedo run, though by now he didn't reckon at all on getting it. The skipper wasn't going to sink the troop transport and that was all that was left. You couldn't use tin fish against aircraft. . . .

When the spread was thick enough and widespread enough Cameron took the *Caithness* round under full wheel to plunge back into it and in effect get lost. When that happened the muck was everywhere, in eyes, mouths, noses and all around the speeding ship. In their vicinity the visibility was down to nil and they were running blind.

'Hope the bridge knows just where that transport is,' Mr Clinch said to his LTO.

'Wide enough berth at the start, sir,' Inman answered. Each time he opened his mouth to speak or breathe, the muck swirled down his throat and left a raw feeling and a foul taste. He rubbed at his eyes, also red and raw. The Gunner(T) was right: funny things happened at sea, and ships could come up close in a very short time if you didn't watch out. However, the radar would be keeping a watch and would alert the bridge pronto, always assuming it was working at full efficiency. The radar aerial had been damaged when the director went but the radio mechanic had carried out running repairs to the best of his ability and so far as Inman knew the set was working. Inman, lost in the pouring smoke, had nothing to do currently, nothing to do but think and worry, and his worry was mostly about home rather than his own predicament under the Jap bombs, which were still coming down in an attempt to knock out the *Caithness*. If one of those bombs had his number on it, it would find him and that was that, no use worrying. If it hadn't, he would live to carry on the bloody war, day after day, week after week, year after year. Inman was beginning to feel he had never known anything in his life but war, and sinkings, and death by blast or drowning. It was all a far cry from the peace-time days of manoeuvres between the Home and Mediterranean Fleets, plenty of time ashore in Gibraltar or Malta or Alexandria . . . foreign commissions China-side or Singapore, or the light cruisers of the West Indies Squadron taking you to exotic places you'd never have seen if you hadn't joined the Andrew. Soft, moonlit nights on watch at anchor beneath the awnings of a fleet at peace, or soft music from the Royal Marine band on the quarterdeck of a battleship when the wardroom was giving a dance for the local talent in Pompey or Guz, bugles, Colours and Sunset . . . no bombs, no Japs or Jerries or Eyeties except as comic figures, foreigners to be more or less scorned by the British Navy's lucky lads, the lads in Navy blue as the old song – before Inman's time – had had it.

And home. Home with a very big H, for Leading Seaman Inman had always been a home lover in spite of having gone to sea and was now a family man, wife and three lovely kids, all still small and two of them twins, and all now shifted out from Pompey and living with the wife's parents in Wales, where it was said to be safe enough. Very nice too: cows and fields and all that, little streams running down from the hills, buttercups growing in their season, and daisies, all a bit different from Commercial Road and Queen Street, the latter with its dozens of pubs and knocking-shops and the raucous shouts of petty officers coming across the barrack wall from the parade ground. . . .

Leading Seaman Inman was thinking of buttercups and daisies and the kids making daisy chains when the *Caithness* came to the end of the smokescreen and ran out into bright sunshine. Inman's luck was out: a Jap dive-bomber came down, handily positioned for its strike, and bright flashes like Christmas-party sparklers coming from its machine-guns. The bombs missed once again but the machine-gun bullets found their mark in Inman's body and left it neatly pock-marked all the way along the back from the neck down.

ii

Caithness was back in the smoke.

'They'll pull out soon, won't they, sir?' Tillotson asked from the murk that covered the bridge.

Cameron nodded. 'That's what I'm reckoning on, Mid. They must have dropped their bomb loads by now.'

'It's some while since the last one, sir.'

'Yes.' Cameron was about to add a further comment when the report came up from the radar cabinet: more aircraft were coming in. This time from the west.

'The Barracudas and Fulmars,' Cameron said, his voice showing excitement and relief. 'Pass to the engine-room, stop making smoke.'

The message went down to Henty. In the boiler-room Tallis closed a number of his injectors. At once the out-pouring from the funnel lessened and the *Caithness* drew clear of the smoke. Cameron said, 'Wheel amidships, Mid. Steer three-six-oh degrees.'

All the bridge personnel were scanning the skies as the smoke fell away astern. Cameron spotted the incoming aircraft, saw the Japs turn away as though uncertain. The Fulmars detached from the Barracudas and gave chase, guns spitting towards the Rising Suns. A light began winking from the leading torpedo-bomber: was the transport to be sunk?

'Answer, no, and get that across fast,' Cameron said to the leading signalman now acting as yeoman. 'Add, explanations will follow.'

He put his glasses on to the bearing of the troop transport; she was turning away to run for it and her guns were silent now, but she would have some light ack-ack stuff to use if the

Barracudas looked like going into an attack. For the time being they were holding off outside the transport's likely range. Cameron passed orders to the midshipman to bring the destroyer round to close the other vessel and then gave the leading signalman his further message for the Barracuda leader. He said, 'Make by light, expect enemy surface reinforcement at any time. Would be glad if you would remain to the limit of your fuel endurance. Intend moving for Trincomalee with transport under escort at best possible speed.'

This message was passed and acknowledged: the Barracudas would comply.

Cameron wiped sweat and filth from a blackened face. He was about to send down for the First Lieutenant when Main appeared at the head of the ladder.

'Here at last,' Main said.

'They didn't lose any time, Number One. Now, I'm going to overhaul the Jap – '

'How long d'you suppose the Barracudas can hang about, sir? To say nothing of the Fulmars.' There was a hint in the First Lieutenant's tone and words that suggested Cameron was hoping for the impossible. 'Their fuel capacity isn't – '

'I know all that, Number One. C-in-C will know the score from my original message. So will the parent carrier, which-ever it is – one of the fleet carriers anyway. I'm hopeful they'll steam eastwards towards us. If the gap's narrowed, the squadron and the fighters can return for re-fuelling when necessary and then be flown off to rejoin us.'

Main said dourly, 'Well, of course, hope springs eternal.'

'Yes, it does.' Cameron's voice was sharp, sharper than he had intended, and Main flushed beneath the filth on his face. Cameron went on before the First Lieutenant could say anything further, 'Now, the transport. I'll use the loud-hailer when I'm within range . . . I'll pass orders for her to head westerly, and tell her I'll be ready to open fire if she doesn't comply. I'll also have the Barracudas as a threat.'

'It's an empty one, sir. The Japs'll know that.'

143

'I wouldn't be too sure. The Jap mind doesn't work like ours. They wouldn't hesitate to put their own men in danger. They can't bank on it that we wouldn't. To them, war's war no matter what.'

'Don't forget their warrior code. They'll fight. There simply isn't any doubt about that.'

'Then we'll be forced to fight too, Number One.'

'I think it's insane, sir. We haven't a hope of bringing it off. You must see that!'

'So what do you suggest? Head for Trinco, and forget it?' Main scowled. 'I didn't say that.'

'No, you didn't. But it's the only inference I can draw.' Cameron took a deep breath, looked around the horizons, as yet clear of any other enemy ships. 'I'm going in, Number One.'

'What are you going to do when you get there?' Main asked.

'I'll take it as it comes. I may put a party aboard – but we'll see how it shapes up. In the meantime, have an armed party of seamen mustered ready under the GI and the seaboat's crew standing by.'

iii

'Disagreement on the bridge, I reckon,' Able Seaman Urridge said. 'Jimmy's got a face like thunder, doesn't like what the skipper's going to do and no more do I, come to that.' The pipe had already gone round the ship and along with the chief bosun's mate Petty Officer Jago was organizing the muster of a boarding party, a case of you and you and you – and one of them was Urridge; another was Roebuck, now nothing but an encumbrance to his gun's crew and safer where Jago could keep a personal eye on him. The seaboat's crew of the watch had been called away and were standing by their boat with the gripes slipped and the boat itself swung out on the davits. Urridge was speaking to Stripey Gizzard, who was still self-conscious about what his stomach had achieved in the

144

tiller flat and felt in need of a friend. Stripey hadn't much time for Urridge normally, not liking sea lawyers, but now he agreed with what Urridge said.

'Asking for it, skipper is. All the same. . . .'

'All the same what, Stripey?'

Gizzard gestured ahead towards the transport, looming larger but still not firing. 'Them pongoes.'

'Stuff the pongoes,' Urridge said, then saw the look on Gizzard's face, the look of warning. He said nothing further but it was already too late: turning in response to Gizzard's expression and a feeling of danger in rear, he saw Petty Officer Jago.

Jago said, 'What was that, Urridge?'

'Nothing, GI.'

'Nothing my arse! I heard you. And anything worse I never did hear, so help me God. You should be bloody ashamed of yourself, Able Seaman Urridge – '

'Didn't mean no 'arm, GI.'

'Oh, no! No harm. Just thinking of yourself as usual – up ladder, Jack, that's you, and bugger everyone else.' Jago lifted a hand and tapped Urridge on the chest. 'I'll be watching you, right?'

Jago marched away. Urridge watched him with dislike. Some people were all for it, dead keen. Not him. Urridge's motto had always been: never volunteer for anything. He never did; but he got lurked in just the same under the you-and-you principle and it wasn't fair. In any case he believed the skipper was doing the wrong thing. Why bother to put a party aboard, put men in danger when the Japs must surely see they'd had it, what with the destroyer's guns and the presence above of torpedo-bombers that could finish the transport off in seconds once they were ordered in? Stood to reason that was the best way. The only way in Urridge's view. You could spend too long worrying about the safety of pongoes.

Aboard the *Yokosuka Maru* there was tension along the troop decks, the prison decks as in effect they were. The armed guards were jumpy, trigger-happy now to the *n*th degree. The British prisoners of war were being circumspect, giving the guards no excuse to use their guns, keeping their heads down and their tongues still, but the atmosphere was that of the knife-edge. They had been given no news at all and with all the deadlights secured over the scuttles they could see nothing of the world outside or what was going on. But they had ears and they could interpret sounds. No one could mistake the gunfire or the fact that it meant British warships in the close vicinity; and there had been the aircraft and the racket of the dive-bombing-Jap aircraft. Then the cessation, and the sound of other, different aircraft that dropped no bombs.

Guesswork came easily enough: the transport, whose engines were working overtime and causing a heavy vibration throughout the ship, was in for it but the forces outside were holding off. Reason obvious: themselves, the helpless prisoners. The fact of them alone might let the Japs off the hook. Whoever was in command of the warships might decide the chances of life even in a Jap prison camp, with eventual release when the war was over, were better than certain death in a sinking. Death for most of them, anyway. Some might get away with it; but not many, because it was not just the hazards of the sea: few of the soldiers doubted that the moment things went awry for the Japs, there would be wholesale and instant slaughter along the prison deck. A natural thought was running through the mind of the senior British officer, a brigadier: how could they assist the navy?

Not a hope; not yet. Currently, one move could start the killing. The Japs wouldn't be taking chances. But a time might come. The brigadier didn't in fact place much hope in success. Had he been with his own battalion of infantry, men who had fought together as a unit, had suffered together in Changi gaol and understood each other's reactions and who would anticipate decisions and orders and act as one under their NCOs, something might have been possible even if only as a result of that comradship leading to a kind of rapport. But as it was the men in the *Yokosuka Maru* were from a vast number of units and corps: infantry, artillery, ordnance, RASC, sappers, even a brace of padres and some doctors. They were not cohesive. It would be a case of each man for himself and that would be suicide.

The tension was not confined to the prisoners: there was anxiety and confusion on the bridge. The master, Captain Keizo Sawano, conferred with his own officers and the officers of the Emperor's military forces.

'We must continue on our course away, and run,' he had said, and said firmly. There had been argument on this point but Captain Sawano remained adamant. He was in command, not the military. He was responsible for his ship and crew. No, he could not hope to outrun the British destroyer, especially with the damage to his bow, but he believed that assistance would come, and come naturally from the east, and he must endeavour to move closer towards it while the British dithered. That they were dithering was obvious, he said. They would not wish to kill their own soldiers unnecessarily, perhaps, he added, unconsciously coming close to Main's prognostications. There was a softness about the British, who were unlike the Japanese.

'They will not give up a valuable prize to save their soldiers, Captain.' This was the military commander, a small man with glittering, pig-like eyes and a sword that almost reached his chin. 'That is not the way wars are won. Very soon the destroyer will again open fire. We should not be seen to run away. In any case,' he added sneeringly, 'they are already overtaking us.'

'Yes, Colonel, they are overtaking us,' Captain Sawano said shortly. Soldiers were always dogmatic and arrogant. Captain Sawano moved to the port wing of his bridge; even to run was in fact pointless unless a Japanese warship appeared as if by magic over the horizon in the next few minutes. Even when undamaged the *Yokosuka Maru* was capable of little more than seventeen knots; the British destroyer could achieve more than thirty. Sawano watched the warship closing by leaps and bounds and suffered the nagging tongue of Colonel Hara and within the next half-hour he heard a loud voice booming at him across the water as the destroyer came up fast and close on his port beam, with her guns trained towards him.

v

Into the loud-hailer Cameron called, 'Stop your engines immediately, and order your guns' crews away from their guns.' Sporadically, and uselessly, the transport had fired her after 6-inch again as they closed. 'If you do not, I shall blow them off their mountings.' He was taking a chance on English being spoken on the transport's bridge. If it was not, he would take no risks: Petty Officer Jago, waiting to board if the order came, was meantime ready to open fire, point of aim the enemy guns. At the current range he couldn't miss, and he was by now as trigger-happy as the armed guards aboard the transport. His own belief was that Cameron should open without further delay. Disarmed, under the guns of the *Caithness* and the presence, for so long as their fuel held out anyway, of the Barracudas and Fulmars, the transport could be herded west without much difficulty until she came under the umbrella of British Naval units out of Trincomalee. Probably they wouldn't even need to put the armed party aboard; though that would be extra insurance, the absence of the men would leave the *Caithness* very short of hands, what with the casualties already sustained.

A leading seaman approached, reported the party mustered and ready. 'What's going to happen, GI?'

'Dunno yet. We'll be told – ' He broke off as he heard Cameron on the loud-hailer, and the Japanese response. 'Listen,' he said.

All along the upper deck, the hands listened to the

148

amplified conversation. The Japanese captain sounded excited and under pressure. 'I have stopped my engines,' he called across the gap. 'But my guns remain.'

'I give you two minutes to withdraw your guns' crews, Captain. At the end of that time, my gunners will open fire.'

'Then I shoot too. With bigger guns.'

'And with knobs on,' Jago murmured. 'Looks like it's going to be a simple case of who presses the tit first.' He fell silent again as Cameron made further use of the loud-hailer, reminding the Japanese captain of the presence of the aircraft.

'A signal by lamp will bring them in,' Cameron called. 'In the meantime, I'm counting. One hundred and twenty seconds starting now.'

There was a silence after that, broken only by Cameron's voice steadily counting as the second hand moved round his wristwatch, a silence from the sea and the guns, with the aircraft circling distantly. There seemed to be a good deal of chatter going on aboard the transport, her own officers conferring with khaki-clad Japanese. There was a flurry of polite bows, and the flash of steel as a sword was waved. Cameron's count had reached one hundred and ten when the loud-hailer came on again from the *Yokosuka Maru*.

'British Captain. . . .'

Cameron flicked his switch. 'Listening.'

'You make threats. We too make threats.'

'What sort of threats?'

'British soldiers in troop decks. They will be shot if you open fire.'

'You'd do that to prisoners of war under your protection?'

'Yes. For sake of Emperor, and own honour.'

On the upper deck Jago said hoarsely, 'Own honour my arse! Dirty little bastards.' He spat over the side. The Jap was speaking again and Jago listened, his face hard.

'First to be shot as example and proof is now being brought to bridge.'

From all the exposed positions along the *Caithness* the

149

hands watched in growing horror and with a feeling of sheer helplessness as an armed party was seen moving for'ard along the transport's embarkation deck, four Japanese soldiers with an NCO in rear, and a British officer in the centre between the files. As the party reached the open wing of the bridge Cameron, through his binoculars, recognized the rank badges of a brigadier. The face was emaciated and deeply lined and the rest of the body was little more than a skeleton. But the Brigadier's back was straight; and as he faced towards the great battle ensign still floating on an occasional movement of air over the decks of the *Caithness*, he brought his hand to the salute.

Once again the loud-hailer spoke across the blue, sun-drenched water. 'You see, British Captain. Many lives are now in your hands. The decision is yours.'

13

MAIN WAS on the bridge with Cameron. He said, 'Well, what now, sir?'

'I don't know, Number One.'

'Cleft stick,' Main said.

'There has to be an answer somewhere.'

'Yes. Break off. It's all we can do.'

'I have an idea that Brigadier wouldn't agree.'

'He's not the only one concerned, is he? I doubt if the troops below decks want to die.' Main studied the transport through Tillotson's binoculars. Impassive-faced Japanese stood at the guns, the 6-inch and an array of close-range weapons in the bridge wing and along the boat deck. They could rake the destroyer from stem to stern; and the *Caithness* could do the same thing back to them. 'Looks like stalemate, sir. They're probably doing the same as us.'

'Which is?'

Main shrugged. 'Waiting for support.'

'Ours is here.' Cameron waved a hand towards the Barracudas. 'But not for much longer. When they haul off. . . .' He left the rest unsaid. Everyone knew the score well enough. When the torpedo-bombers and fighters reached the safe limit of their fuel, it would be the one ship against the other, and the British troops the pawns in the middle, waiting for the Japanese machine-guns to mow them down. No way out . . . except the First Lieutenant's and

151

Cameron could never bring himself to steam tamely away, watched by the straight-backed, exhausted Brigadier, and leave the prisoners to the fate of being used as a labour force, building a railway in the name of the Rising Sun.

Not to be thought of; but, as Main had said, what else was there? His threat had been countered, and by a much more effective one. He should have thought of that; but even if he had done so, the result would have remained. Main had spoken of waiting for support to arrive. It was anybody's guess whose support would turn up first – if any did at all. If it didn't then both he and the *Yokosuka Maru* appeared doomed to sit it out indefinitely. But it was pretty certain that a Japanese force, air or surface, would in fact have been despatched by now. . . .

One thing piled upon another: there was the flash of a lamp from the Barracuda leader and Cameron's acting yeoman read off a signal: 'Am returning to base with Fulmars to refuel. Will be back soonest possible.'

'Acknowledge,' Cameron said briefly. He sent up a prayer that the refuelling parties would be ready aboard the carrier, ready to connect up the moment the aircraft picked up the trip-wires on the flight deck and no snags. Even minutes could count now; and in fact it would be more like hours before the air cover came back. Now the planes were turning, heading back to the west, leaving a very naked feeling in their wake. Cameron, coming to a decision on one matter, took up the sound-powered telephone to the wardroom flat. 'Surgeon Lieutenant on the bridge,' he said when it was answered. When Styles came up at the double, he told him to encypher a signal for Trincomalee. He said, 'It's all we can do now, for what it's worth, doc. Refer back to my previous signal . . . the message runs: "Am in close contact with Japanese transport carrying British POWs under threat if I intervene. Distant support requested to counter likely enemy reinforcements but suggest caution in POW interest." All right, doc? I'll give you our position from the chart – add it to the signal.' He passed the ship's position. 'Fast as you can.'

Styles promised speed and went down the ladder. Cameron, struck by a sudden idea, almost called him back but decided not to. His thought had been to do with the Japanese prisoner who'd crash landed on the fo'c'sle earlier: that Jap could perhaps be used as a kind of hostage, an eye for an eye if the British aboard the transport were made to suffer, but it didn't take long for the idea to be dismissed. It would never impress the Japanese officers, a prisoner was already dishonoured and in any case Styles wouldn't wear it, it would be unethical and against the Geneva Convention. . . From the forebridge Cameron and Tillotson looked out towards the helpless Brigadier. He, too, would be in a cleft stick. He might well be wanting to shout across that his own life was not to be considered; but he wouldn't want to precipitate the opening of the machine-guns along the troop decks. He was as stymied as Cameron.

Main said, 'There's one thing certain. We haven't a hope of getting a boarding party across now.'

'Keep them handy just the same, Number One. The time may come.'

'Not this side of heaven.'

Cameron wasn't listening: he was staring across towards the transport's damaged bow, the plating torn back, the fo'c'sle with its slight dip. The water would be washing up against the collision bulkhead, surging against it through the opened stem. If the collision bulkhead went, the sea would gain entry and bring the big ship farther down by the head, pour throughout the ship . . . liners had their watertight bulkheads, of course, but were not compartmented to the same extent as warships and the giving way of the collision bulkhead, the ship's principal line of defence against flooding, would put her in immediate danger of sinking.

Cameron pondered: there would be something like desperation in the act he was considering and he couldn't hope to save all the British troops, but it seemed to him the only way. He said, 'How about sending them to panic stations, Number One?'

153

'Panic stations, sir?'

'Start the sinking process.'

'Open fire? I thought that was – '

'In a special sense, one particular spot. Shatter the collision bulkhead, Number One! If they began to go down, I'll bet they wouldn't be hanging about below decks – the guards, I mean. It could give the troops a chance. Some of them, anyway. A chance to break out and jump for it.'

Main shook his head. 'Wouldn't work. They'd batten down the troop-deck hatches.'

'Not if the troops ticked over and took their chance on rushing the guards in time. It's the only way I can see.'

'That Brigadier – '

'I know. First to go. You needn't tell me.'

'So?'

'We have a hell of a lot of men to think about, Number One. And the loss of a transport might even make the Japs change their minds about further Burma drafts. Even for the Japs, ships don't grow on trees.'

Main said, 'It's cold-blooded.'

'It's war, Number One. I hate it as much as you do. And they're all going to a living death, the Brigadier included. They might even prefer this way. And we may not have much time left.'

Main shrugged. 'It's your decision, sir.'

'Yes,' Cameron said, 'I know.' He moved across to the after end of the bridge. Mr Clinch was visible, down by the tubes on the starboard side. Torpedo attack could be more effective than the guns. Cameron called to him, and he looked up, lifted a hand in acknowledgment.

'On the bridge, please, Mr Clinch,' Cameron said, and the Gunner(T) came aft at the trot.

ii

Once again Cameron used the loud-hailer, engaging the Japanese captain in conversation while Mr Clinch made ready on the port side, shielded from the enemy's eyes by the midship superstructure. In the engine-room the engineer officer and Chief ERA Trigg were standing by to move the engines over at dead slow. Cameron's voice went across the water.

'We have reached deadlock, Captain.'

'Dead-lock?'

'An impasse.'

'Impasse?'

It didn't matter what he said so long as the Japanese were kept occupied until Mr Clinch reported ready, which he should do at any moment. 'We have each uttered threats.'

'Yes.'

Cameron brought up his binoculars, focused on the Brigadier. The soldier's face was impassive, giving nothing away. He would have a family most probably, somewhere back across the seas in England. Cameron was about to shatter their lives as well as the Brigadier's. But duty had to be done. When you caught the enemy, you used every endeavour to sink him, and you never let any one man's life stand in the way. All this, Cameron knew. But it didn't go any way at all towards lightening the burden of conscience. He was about to call something else across the water when the sound-powered telephone whined from the port torpedo-tubes and Clinch's voice reported.

'All ready, sir.'

'Right.' Cameron moved to the port wing of the bridge and looked down. Mr Clinch had his orders and could be relied on to carry them out. Cameron took the ship from the midshipman and passed his own orders to the wheelhouse.

'Engines dead slow ahead, wheel hard-a-starboard.'

Chapman repeated the order back and put the helm hard over. Imperceptibly at first, the *Caithness* began to swing in response to her rudder as the thrust of the screws put way on her. In the wheelhouse Chapman lit a cigarette and inhaled deeply, blew the smoke out again in a cloud. He found his hands were trembling a little on the wheel as he waited for the

155

Captain's next order, which would be to put the helm amidships. Almost immediately after that the world would come to a sudden end for an unspecified number of men, British and Jap, aboard the transport and probably all hell would be let loose against the destroyer as the Jap opened on a very close target, almost a sitting one until the skipper ordered more speed, Chapman thought. It was going to be very, very chancy, and very, very nasty while it lasted. . . .

'Midships!'

'Midships, sir.' Chapman released the wheel, letting it spin back. 'Wheel's amidships, sir.'

On the bridge Cameron nodded at the midshipman, standing by to pass the word aft. 'Fire when ready,' he said. Down by the tubes, as the *Caithness* steadied with her port side now visible to the Japanese and the tubes nicely lined up on the transport's stem, it was Mr Clinch who gave the final order.

'*Fire one!*'

There was a plop and a hiss and a tin fish dropped into the water and sped for the transport's gaping bow plates. At such close range you couldn't miss, Mr Clinch knew. He put his hands over his ears. One of the torpedomen spat over the side behind the torpedo, set just below the surface and running very nicely, its trail moving inexorably for its target. The firing must obviously have been visible from the transport, but so far there had been no reaction. Not that there was anything the Japs could do about it, Mr Clinch thought, just sit there and take it, that was all, no time left. Any moment now. . . .

The aim had been true enough: the world seemed to burst about Mr Clinch's ears when the torpedo impacted. There was a vast explosion, streaks of flame and a lot of smoke and kerfuffle, and at once the transport's bow went down. The ship seemed to lurch for a moment to port and then straightened, now with the whole of the bow section deep under water and the sea rising up along the fo'c'sle almost back to the superstructure and the stern lifting high. There was panic on her bridge, officers shouting and running down the ladders like lunatics, and members of the crew pouring from the hatches from the lower decks. It was obvious enough that the objective had been achieved, the collision bulkhead shattered.

She wasn't going to last long.

On the upper deck the First Lieutenant, with the chief bosun's mate, was organizing the nets, hung over the side for the pick-up of the survivors. On the transport's bridge, the Brigadier had taken advantage of the panic and emaciated as he was had managed to free himself of his armed escort and even to grab for one of their guns; and he could be seen from the destroyer's bridge now, backing away behind the barrel of an automatic rifle. A few moments after this Cameron saw the khaki drill uniforms emerging in a mass from companionways fore and aft.

He shouted to them to jump. As he did so the Japanese close-range gunners opened from the transport's boat deck, sending a rain of bullets down the side, aiming at the jumping British soldiers and the open decks of the *Caithness*. Cameron, now bringing his ship in close for the benefit of the swimming men, came inside the angle of depression of the 6-inch guns, rendering them unable to bear. His own close-range weapons swept the side of the transport, forcing the crew and guards back, and arced upwards towards the bridge whenever a Japanese face was seen. Blood began to run down the vessel's side plating, and two bodies hung from a set of davits, heads down, feet entangled in the rope falls as the bullets took them. Already soldiers were climbing the destroyer's nets and being assisted aboard by the seamen: too many for a count, though Petty Officer Bustacle did his best to keep some sort of check so as to be able to report to the bridge just how overloaded they were going to be. Dozens and dozens of them – hundreds as the minutes passed, turning the *Caithness* into a floating sardine tin, pongoes everywhere, trying to dodge the bullets coming from the transport, putting bulkheads between themselves and the enemy wherever possible.

Then a stream of automatic fire came from the Brigadier on the transport's bridge, firing aft, and more bodies toppled from the boat decks, Japanese bodies. The close-range fire on the *Caithness* faltered and then died away. By now the big ship was farther down in the water, bows well under and the superstructure beginning to ride like a submarine awash.

There was a shout from her bridge, and Cameron looked up, waved an arm: the Brigadier, his uniform torn and bloodied, was standing in the bridge wing and alongside him, grinning like demons, were three more British soldiers. 'All over,' the Brigadier called. 'We have control of what's left.'

'Better jump now, sir – '

'I'm about to, Captain. Then I suggest you move out. She's not going to last much longer, or am I teaching my grand-mother?' The Brigadier didn't wait any longer: with his three companions he climbed the rail of the bridge wing and dived in. He struck out and drifted closer until he could be taken by the ship's company manning the nets. Cameron waited as long as he dared; troops were still coming over the side, though not in such large numbers now. He looked along his decks, fore and aft. There was literally no space left. Khaki drill was everywhere, tight-packed on the open decks, on the superstructure, around the guns, all over the fo'c'sle and even up the bridge ladders. It was going to be virtually impossible to fight his ship, at least until the brown jobs had been sorted out into some sort of order and, like cargo, stowed neatly away.

The end was not far off now; the transport was sliding by the second, she must be completely flooded below. Cameron watched, delaying until the last possible moment, the moment when to hold on for the final few would be to put all the others in danger of being drawn into the whirlpool that would be created by the sinking of a former liner. And where was Main? He should have been about the decks, seeing to the trim: too many men had been clustered on the starboard side away from the firing earlier, and their sheer weight was giving the *Caithness* an unhandy list.

Cameron took up the Tannoy. 'First Lieutenant to report to the bridge. Chief bosun's mate?'

From just for'ard of the bridge Bustacle called up. 'Here, sir!'

Cameron leaned over the screen. 'Get her trimmed, buffer.'

'Doing me best, sir.'

'Where's the First Lieutenant?'

'Dunno, sir. Haven't seen him, sir.'

Frowning, Cameron stepped back to the binnacle. A quick look round – still men swimming for the nets. Give them a shade longer . . . but suddenly the transport started a rush. Cameron used the Tannoy again, loudly over the water. 'I'm about to put the engines ahead so as to haul clear as she goes. All swimmers stand clear of the screws. I'll float a grass line aft. Grab it if you can and I'll tow you clear.' Then he bent to the voice-pipe as the grass line was trailed out astern. 'Wheel hard-a-port, engines full ahead.'

They wouldn't all make it. Some were going to be churned up by the flail of the twin propellers beneath the counter. Cameron felt as though he were sweating blood. But he had been only just in time. As the *Caithness* slid away under full power, now with the helm amidships, the *Yokosuka Maru* went into her death throes, going down fast by the bow, her stern lifting high and cascading living and dead Japanese down her many decks until she vanished completely beneath the water in a gush of steam and smoke and a mighty roaring sound as the sea rushed in to fill the gap. Cameron felt the back-pull, felt the way come off his ship as the water surged and tugged him towards the maelstrom. Then, as the thrust of his engines overcame the pull, he was away and clear.

When the close-range weapons had started up Main had dived for cover, down the ladder to the wardroom flat. Able Seaman Urridge had seen him go; Ordinary Seaman Roebuck had not.

'But you don't bloody say so,' Urridge said. 'All right?'

'What d'you mean?'

'You know what I mean, son. You know very well. Jimmy did a bunk. We're witnesses. You and me both.'

'Telling lies – '

'Bollocks! Keep to the story and we've got him. You know what 'appened in the tiller flat. Now he'll get his deserts, if you keep your 'ead.'

'You going to report it, then?'

'Probably. Or the skipper may ask.'

'He won't do that.'

'Who says so? Jimmy's been missing right through. Skipper's bound to make enquiries, see? That's when we comes in. Till then, keep it to yourself.'

Roebuck didn't respond. He didn't like it at all. Officers always won out in the end. Anyway, Jimmy would have an explanation to offer when asked, bound to have. Urridge had said Jimmy had gone to ground like a streak of lightning the moment the first bullets zipped across. Well, maybe he had; but he would find a way of covering up . . . meanwhile Urridge was rabbiting on about pongoes, pongoes everywhere, cluttering up the messdecks and stores, littering the galley flat and the wardroom flat, packed tight like fleas all along the upper deck, hanging on where they could as the destroyer rolled to the beginnings of a swell and moved at high speed for Trincomalee. Those lying in heaps along the messdecks would soon, Urridge said, turn into puke-producing units and make the place stink to heaven. The buzz had gone round the ship that the buffer had reported to the skipper that the best count he'd been able to make was upwards of eleven hundred men embarked and no one seemed to know for sure how many had been aboard the transport, how many had died. Not that it made any difference now. The dead were dead and that was that. It was the living they had to worry about. And a fat lot of hope they would have of ever seeing Trinco, Urridge said, when the Japs caught up with them.

14

URRIDGE WAS back to duty as wardroom messman, once again in charge in the pantry. The wardroom itself was a shambles, filled to overflowing with pongo officers and more outside in the flat, falling over each other as they lay on the deck or got up to go to the heads or try to reach the ladder and make the open air before they were seasick. The First Lieutenant was still trying to sort things out and not achieving much, Urridge reckoned.

Useless sod.

Urridge reflected, looking through the hatch into the wardroom, on what he'd recently been told by Roebuck, who'd got it from the starboard bridge lookout, another OD. The skipper had asked Jimmy a few pointed questions, all friendly of course, and Jimmy had made something of a joke of it. Just before the destroyer had hauled off from the transport he'd gone below to the wardroom flat to ensure a gangway was kept open between the refuge-seeking troops, a gangway for the essential movements of the ship's company to and from vital spaces. In so doing, he'd found himself hemmed in by the press of bodies coming down the ladder and hadn't been able to make it back on deck.

'Skipper believe it?' Urridge had asked.

'Don't know. Anyway, he wouldn't call Jimmy a liar in front of ratings, would he?'

Of course he wouldn't. Officers were officers, they didn't

fall out in front of the peasants on the lower deck. Fair enough, perhaps. But not if Jimmy was going to get away with it where a rating wouldn't. Urridge had the evidence of his own eyes and knew the First Lieutenant had spent the whole of the action in the safety of the wardroom flat. If he'd been seen skulking, he'd very likely have come up with a load of bullshit about damage control.

Urridge came away from the hatch and delved into a cupboard beneath a working surface that ran the length of the wardroom bulkhead. He brought up a bottle labelled Lea and Perrin's Worcestershire Sauce, the label having once been genuine but no longer descriptive of the contents: the bottle contained rum, not the two-water grog as issued to ratings below PO, but neaters. Urridge had an understanding with the leading supply assistant responsible under the Coxswain for the rum issue and in charge of the barricoes from which the daily issue was drawn. How the LSA squared his depredations with the 'Swain Urridge didn't know and didn't care; it was enough that he got what he wanted in exchange for liberal helpings of the officers' nosh.

Urridge took a swig, wiped the back of a hand across his lips, and felt a sight better. He was lighting a fag when the Tannoy came on and Cameron's voice announced distant radar contact with the enemy.

ii

The contact was bearing dead astern – from the east. That could only mean the Japs were coming up. Surface attack: three ships, the report had said. Not much time had in fact passed since the troops had been embarked and the transport had gone down; so far the British air umbrella had not returned.

Cameron and Mr Clinch scanned the seas astern. The Gunner(T) had been co-opted into the bridge watchkeeping rota, now sadly short on account of the casualties. So far there was nothing to be seen. Within half a minute of the Tannoy

163

announcement Main and the Brigadier had reached the bridge. Cameron said he didn't intend going to action stations yet; there was time in hand and the ship's company was tired to the point of exhaustion. He asked, 'What about the troops, Number One?'

'I'm getting as many of them below as possible, sir. The seamen's and stokers' messdecks are just about cram full.'

Cameron nodded, then turned to the Brigadier. 'Sorry about this, sir – '

'Hardly your fault, is it?'

Cameron gave a tight grin. 'No. But – '

'Yes, I know what you mean, old chap. My men are going to be sitting targets, those who can't get below. It can't be helped and that's all about it. I should be apologizing for cluttering up your action decks.' The soldier staggered a little; he hadn't got his sea-legs, and looked to Cameron as weak as a kitten in any case.

Cameron said, 'I suggest you go below yourself, sir.'

'No, no. . . .'

'You need rest, sir.'

'No, I'm staying here. So long as I'm not in the way, that is.' The Brigadier passed a thin, scrawny hand over his eyes. The blood vessels stood out like purple ropes, like those of a much older man. Cameron thought he was probably not much over forty-five but looked sixty plus. His hair was still dark but was falling out; he looked like a scarecrow in his tattered khaki drill. Soon after he'd been helped aboard from the nets Cameron had had a word with him. There had been tears of relief and gratitude in his eyes and he had pumped Cameron's hand as though he would never let go. It had not been the moment to ask about his treatment as a Japanese POW but questions had in fact been unnecessary: his face and his handshake had told Cameron all he needed to know about the whole military draft, and had vindicated Cameron's action in risking his ship and her company.

Another report from the radar indicated the echoes

closing. By Cameron's calculation of the enemy's speed and the distance, the *Caithness* would be within gun range in two hours or less.

iii

The engine-room had been informed of the facts and Mr Henty had reported all well with his engines though he would need to keep a sharp eye on his bunkers.

'All this maximum revs, sir. Drinks it, it does.'

'Do your best, Chief.'

'I'll do that, sir.' Henty, shoving back the handset of the sound-powered telephone and his cap to the back of his head at the same time, reflected that doing one's best wasn't going to solve the fuel problem. If the bridge ordered maximum revolutions you used up the fuel and that was that, no possible option of economy. When the tanks ran out, you stopped. If the enemy was present, you then got blown out of the hogwash. Or you surrendered, presumably. Three ships against one just didn't work out, but it wasn't often a British ship struck its colours. Mr Henty turned the starting platform over to Chief ERA Trigg and went through to the boiler-room for a word with the stoker PO.

'How's it going, eh, Tallis?'

'All right, sir.'

'Worried about the fuel. . . .'

'We're all right for a while.'

'Not all the way to Trinco, though.'

'Not at this speed, sir, no. You warned the bridge?'

'Course. I don't know what's in the skipper's mind. Maybe he'll ask later on for a tanker to be sent out.'

Tallis said, 'I reckon he could ask for something else right now: assistance, now the Japs are on our arses.'

'You know as well as I do, you don't break wireless silence at sea.'

'He's broken it already, sir, so the buzz says. When he asked for assistance earlier . . . we're not all that far off our

165

position at the time he made that. Wouldn't give anything away, not really, would he?'

Henty didn't answer. That was the skipper's business, not his. But he reckoned Tallis had something. Cameron could make an urgent signal to C-in-C, indicating he was about to come under surface attack. It might ginger up the ruddy Admiral, just might. Admirals, in Henty's view, tended to fight their own wars rather than those of the destroyers. Unless they'd been destroyer men themselves before hoisting their flags in command of the big stuff, they tended to have battleship mentalities and regarded the heavy ships as too bloody valuable to be spared – the concept of the fleet in being, the overriding need to maintain the capital ships in safety to be ever the main threat to the enemy, and that thinking could cover the cruisers as well since they formed the escort to the battleships that formed the fleet.

'And bugger the poor bloody destroyers,' Henty said aloud.

'Beg pardon, sir?'

'Nothing to fret about,' Henty said absently. He went back to the starting platform, thinking other thoughts, faraway ones of home and the missus as he always did just before action. The peace and quiet of the Dorset countryside and the missus pottering about in the garden. She liked looking after gardens, she'd found – never had one before, not till he'd evacuated her after war broke out. She'd proved good with vegetables, and her nice young carrots and broad beans and such were one of the joys of leave to Mr Henty, leave that he hadn't had for much too long now. . . . *This is my story*, Mr Henty hummed to himself amid the din and throb of his engines, *this is my song, We've been in commission too bloody long*. The girls weren't much help, didn't like dirtying their hands with Dorset mud, and come to that they weren't at home any more, not often. Twenty and twenty-two, both of them in the WAAF, both of them with boy-friends of whom Mr Henty didn't approve. RAF they were, and Mr Henty was scathing about the Brylcreem Boys, always had been. He was well aware the young men didn't like him either. A stuffy old-stager, a fuddy-duddy from a ship's engine-room who talked about hanky-panky in a disapproving tone when the girls cuddled on a sofa in the front room.

Well, maybe he wouldn't be a gooseberry to them for much longer. Not once the Japs caught up. He wondered how Tallis was feeling about that. Tallis with his problem of loneliness ashore that could also reach solution before the day was out. Or would it? Mr Henty, automatically keeping his eye on everything inside his thudding, pounding kingdom, recalled that conversation he'd had with Lieutenant Pegram. Pegram, he'd believed you survived death in a very positive form, not the body but the spirit, and that the spirit remained more or less on earth, dodging about at will and, like himself currently, keeping an eye on things though in the spirit's case without the power to bawl someone out and put wrongs to rights. Now that, Mr Henty thought, could be very frustrating for those with problems left behind on earth. If, as Pegram had seemed to suggest, you stayed put after death in a different and invisible form, it could be a sort of hell. Seeing the girls doing things that he could no longer object to, seeing them marry their RAF erks, seeing the missis grow older and older till she could no longer fend for herself. Hovering about and no one knowing you were there. It would be the same – according to Lieutenant Pegram's theories – if you were blown to little pieces by a projy or a bomb. Your spirit wouldn't scatter . . . it would be a funny feeling, to remain absolutely intact soulwise and be aware of your body all flying apart away from you.

iv

The bottle that had once held Worcestershire Sauce was nearly empty. Urridge blinked through bleary eyes and lurched against the wardroom ice-box, standing in a corner of the pantry. He drained the bottle and moved with a degree of uncertainty in his gait towards the cupboard. There was

167

another bottle, vinegar this time, also filled with full-strength rum. Urridge gave a belch and reached into the cupboard. Somewhat dimly he heard the Tannoy come on and the skipper's voice spoke from it. Something about the enemy closing, a warning that the ship's company would go to action stations within the next five minutes. Then the Tannoy clicked off and Urridge became aware of disturbance outside the pantry, in the flat. The pongoes were milling about and someone was shouting orders.

Jimmy.

Urridge slid the pantry door open and there, sure enough, was the First Lieutenant, pushing through the mob. Urridge swayed unsteadily and as Main came past him he said in a thick voice, 'Skulking again, eh.'

The First Lieutenant stopped. 'What was that, Urridge?'

'Shit scared, that's you.'

Main flushed. He said, 'You're drunk, Urridge. Drunk on duty, with the ship about to go into action.'

'Not that drunk. . . .'

Main said sharply. 'Into the pantry, Urridge. Move!'

He pushed Urridge backwards, and Urridge sat down suddenly on the deck. The First Lieutenant went in and shut the door. 'Now, Urridge. I'm putting you under arrest for your own protection and in due course you'll be charged with being drunk on rum that shouldn't be in your possession. I – '

'You and who else, eh?' Urridge lurched to his feet, his mind seeming to himself crystal clear and functioning along the lines of his past conversations with Ordinary Seaman Roebuck. This time, he had Jimmy all ends up. Down in the wardroom flat again where he'd have a nice bit of steel bulkhead all around him when the guns opened. 'Tell you something – *sir*. You're an officer, I'm a rating, right? All right for some . . . you wanna charge me, get me put in cells. That's . . . that's where I'll bloody put you an' all. Skulking from action. I see you earlier on . . . pissing off down the wardroom flat. I see you. So did others.' He waved his arms in the air. 'I'll make a report to the skipper, so 'elp me. All right for some. Skipper, 'e knows already what you did in the tiller flat. I reckon you've bloody 'ad it, mate.'

Main stood dumb, his face drained. His mouth opened and shut again. His features seemed to crumple. Urridge stared at him, triumph of a kind showing in his face, a devilish grin of glee and gloating. It didn't last: Urridge had taken a drop too much. He sagged to the deck like a sack of potatoes and lay in a sterterously-breathing heap. The First Lieutenant turned away and left the pantry, closing the door behind him.

v

On the bridge Cameron waited for what looked as if it might be the end. He would fight to a finish: he would not surrender. The Jap revenge on the surrendered troops would be terrible; they would die in any case, but only after humiliation and wicked physical treatment. Cameron had anticipated matters as prognosticated by Stoker PO Tallis down below: already the signal had gone out to Trincomalee, in plain language: 'Am about to come under surface attack with eleven hundred troops embarked.' He had added their position from the chart and that had been all. He hadn't even in so many words requested assistance; that would be up to C-in-C. Cameron knew just what the availability of warships was: bloody little! And C-in-C had other worries than a lone destroyer trying to make it home across the lower reaches of the Bay of Bengal.

How long would he have to wait before he knew?

Those Barracudas and Fulmars – they hadn't come back. Diverted elsewhere, some other emergency? Or their parent carrier sunk by a Jap strike?

Mr Clinch had had another suggestion. 'Rotten navigators, sir. Bad as the RAF. Couldn't find us again.'

'They're not all that bad, Torps.'

'Huh!'

'Anyway . . . try and find something more cheerful to say.'

'Like the Fleet Air Arm song, eh? The makee-learn pilot trying to land on *Formidable*?' Mr Clinch's voice shifted into an attempt at wheezing song. ' "He forgot all the masts that poke up from *Formid*, And a seat in the goofers was worth fifty quid. . . ." '

'Put a sock in it, Torps, for God's sake.'

'Sorry sir.' Mr Clinch sounded injured. 'Just trying to be happy like.'

'Yes, I know. I'm not critizing *you*. Just your voice.'

Cameron watched out astern continually, looking for the give-away smoke. Reports were coming in at intervals from the radar and he was in no doubt that it was a case of any time now. Slowly but surely the echoes were overtaking. Soon after his broadcast over the Tannoy there was a step on the starboard ladder and the First Lieutenant came up. There was something odd in his manner, and Cameron lifted his eyebrows.

'Anything up, Number One?'

'Er . . . up, sir? No.'

'Everything bearing an equal strain?'

'Yes.' Main avoided Cameron's eye. He made no reference to Urridge.

'How are the troops?' The Brigadier had been persuaded by the Surgeon Lieutenant to go below for a spell and Cameron had offered him his own bunk, but he knew the oc Troops would be up on the bridge again as soon as the hands were sent to action stations. 'Good spirits – or not?' Even as he said the words he knew it was a silly question but he wanted to keep Main talking and see if anything emerged.

'I'd say they're just trusting in the navy,' Main said. 'We rescued them, we'll see them home.'

'Something like Dunkirk?'

'Something like that, yes.'

'We'll try not to let them down,' Cameron said. He knew those words were as meaningless as his question. None of them were going to have much hope, and the troops on deck would be lambs to the slaughter.

The radar came up again: 'Enemy distant eleven miles, sir.'

'Thank you. Hands to action stations, Number One.'

The alarm rattlers sounded, urgent and strident throughout the ship. Impeded by the soldiers, the ship's company went to their stations at the guns and tubes, boiler-room and engine-room and tiller flat, all the damage-control positions manned. A matter of minutes later the Japanese warships were in sight, hull down as yet, dark blurs moving into the rays of a brilliantly coloured sunset across an indigo sea. It would not be long before dusk, and following the dusk the swift fall of the dark, the tropic night.

15

Mr Clinch had gone aft to his torpedo-tubes; Midshipman Tillotson had taken over the watch on the bridge. Cameron spoke to the engine-room: if he could keep the *Caithness* outside the effective range of the Japanese guns until after full dark, they might have a better chance.

'Engines are flat out now, sir,' Mr Henty said.

'I know, Chief. Just see if you can squeeze out another couple or so revs.'

'Do me best,' Henty said. Like the old woman who peed in the sea, every little helped, he thought. He passed the word to his Chief ERA, and Trigg said there was some bloody hope, they'd go and sheer the holding-down bolts if they went and flogged the engines any more. But the word spread throughout the engine spaces and in the boiler-room Stoker PO Tallis kept up the fuel injection and prayed they wouldn't run out in the middle of the action. Even Leading Stoker Zebedee was on the ball now, no more moaning. Like them all, Zebedee had hoisted in the fact that it was touch and go, or most likely hit or blow, and the engine-room and boiler-room hands in the worst position of all.

ii

The First Lieutenant, on Cameron's orders, had turned over the damage-control parties to ERA Walsh and was himself

172

acting as officer of the quarters on the guns. He couldn't be everywhere at once but somehow or other that was precisely what Petty Officer Jago managed to achieve – or so it seemed to the guns' crews as they waited for the order to open. Jago moved fast and purposefully from gun to gun, shoving the pongoes aside, making his presence felt, encouraging, cursing, keeping the gunnery rates on their toes and keyed-up to shoot well. Jimmy, the hands noted, was in a dream or something: he moved about like a wet fish ineffectively nit-picking. In point of fact Main was in a state of jitters. His mind was on Able Seaman Urridge, still for all he knew lying in a drunken stupor down below in the wardroom pantry. When he recovered, if any of them were still alive when the action was over, Urridge would have to be charged. When he was charged, he would talk in his own defence, and then Main would have a tough time of it with Cameron, with Captain(D) in Trincomalee, and then with the Board of Admiralty via C-in-C. And there was another point: Urridge shouldn't have been left. The doctor should have been informed, and the man should have been placed under guard, even in the sick bay. There had been dereliction of duty on Main's part in not seeing to that. But there had been no witnesses to the scene in the pantry. . . .

Suddenly, fear swept through Main like a fiery sword: it just didn't matter any more. One ship against three, and the high command safe in Trincomalee seeming totally un-disposed to send out assistance, for which, even if they had, the time had run out. Action would commence at any moment and he was protected against the gunfire by no more than his white anti-flash gear and a steel helmet. It was going to need a miracle and miracles didn't happen very often. On the other hand, a lot of problems would be solved, personal problems and everyone had to die some time. If only –

Main's thoughts were broken into suddenly.

In front of him Petty Officer Jago's harsh voice said, 'All right, sir, are you?'

'I . . . I'm all right.'

'Glad to hear that, sir.'

'Why did you ask?'

'You've a worried look, sir, if I may be so bold.' Jago rose and fell on the balls of his feet, hands clasped behind his back, very much the parade-ground gunner's mate. He coughed. 'Urridge, sir.'

Main started and his face flushed. 'Urridge?'

'Yes, sir, Urridge. Under the weather in the wardroom pantry. I heard a buzz you'd had words with him and that he appeared drunk. I've taken the appropriate action, sir. Thought you'd like to know . . . in the sick bay, he is. Likely to face a stomach pump, I understand.'

Main looked sick himself. 'Thank you, GI.' He paused. 'Was he . . . did he speak at all?'

Jago stared the First Lieutenant in the eyes. 'He uttered a word or two, sir, yes. Slurred like, but understandable.' Before Main could say anything further, Jago turned away towards the after guns. The day grew darker, hiding the expression on the First Lieutenant's face. By now it was not far off full dark. On the bridge Cameron decided, dark or not, that to make smoke might help to throw off the enemy's fire when the guns opened, and he passed the word to the engine-room, thereafter making frequent alterations of course so as to spread the area of smoke and confuse the Japanese gunlayers the more. He was on the starboard tack of his zig-zag when the pursuing ships opened, firing blind into the murk that lay over the water. Along the decks there was a stir among the smoke-blackened troops, a kind of instinctive and collective heads-down against the fall of shot. Cameron, steaming blind now, paced the bridge, two steps one way, two the other. Where the so-and-so was the support from Trinco?

iii

Earlier, on receipt of the signal from the *Caithness*, the naval staff had been called into conference. A good deal of discussion and scrutinizing of charts and the maps showing the disposition of the warships of the Eastern Fleet had followed: there had been divergences of view. The Commander-in-Chief was at sea with the main fleet, to the south of Ceylon. He was too far off the position of the *Caithness* as reported by Cameron, and in any case the Chief of Staff ashore was adamant that no wireless signals should be addressed to the fleet in order to request instructions, thus risking telling the Japanese that they were at sea. It was a decision the Flag Officer in Charge ashore had to make on his own. Tapping the chart with a pencil the Chief of Staff said, 'Well, there you are, sir. No damn ships! Naked as a baby's bottom.'

'Baby's bottoms aren't always naked, Captain. Nor are we.' FOIC lifted a pointer to the big wall map. 'Napkins! Those two cruisers.'

Beneath the pointer were two Colony Class cruisers, *Guiana* and *Brunei*, detached from the fleet. The Chief of Staff said no. They were proceeding south to cover a convoy coming up from the Cape to Bombay and with German U-boats known to be operating off the east coast of Africa, and the likelihood of air strikes out of Madagascar, the additional protection was vital, the Chief of Staff said. There were many more lives at stake in the northbound convoy. It was a question of priorities. FOIC conceded the point but said, 'It's a rotten business, Beale.'

'Yes, sir, it is. But there's really no alternative. Even if we were able to make use of *Guiana* and *Brunei*, they both – '

'Come under the orders of C-in-C. I know that, Beale. It was just a thought. I take your point about not addressing signals – almost certainly the bloody Japs have the call signs.'

'And the Nazis, sir.' Captain Beale paused. 'I know how you feel. I feel the same. Those troops. Hopes raised, and now this.'

'What about that carrier?' FOIC asked.

The Chief of Staff shrugged. 'I've no idea, sir. *Caithness*

175

didn't say anything about air support in the vicinity.'

'It's the last hope,' FOIC said. Nothing had been heard from the aircraft-carrier after the orders had gone out much earlier to fly off aircraft to the assistance of the destroyer; once again, there were the considerations of maintaining wireless silence against the listening antennae of the enemy. So the Naval staff at Trincomalee, like Cameron aboard the *Caithness*, were in ignorance of the facts: the first of the heavy Barracudas to land on for refuelling had misjudged the approach over the round-down aft, had missed the trip-wires laid across the flight deck to catch the hook, had crashed into the barrier and burst into flames The second, following too closely, had attempted to gain height and go round again, but had failed and had crashed into the first. There had been a raging furnace on the flight deck and by the time the fire-fighting parties had it under control the remaining aircraft had come to the end of their fuel and had had to ditch. Only three pilots had been recovered and the carrier was as yet in no position to fly off more aircraft. But – and again this was unknown in Trincomalee – she had altered course towards the last-known position of the *Caithness* as corrected by dead reckoning from her reported course.

iv

The smoke screen in the night was doing its work well: the fall of shot from the Japanese destroyers was all over the place. If anything hit *Caithness*, it would be sheer chance – but the chance was there. The enemy seemed to have opened with all he'd got in the way of something like 4.7s. Before long, Cameron knew he could steam slap into one of the projectiles and when he did that the casualties along the upper deck would be catastrophic with so many tight-packed soldiers wide open to the gunfire. The lower decks were already crammed to capacity: Bustacle had done his best and could do no more. The atmosphere below was horrific; there

176

was the very smell of fear as the crack of the distant guns continued without pause. An NCO was doing his best to cram even more men in, pushing and shoving bodies through the watertight doors so that the last of them was virtually held down himself by the clips when they were wrenched on from outside.

Smoke wreathed chokingly, swirling across the bridge, acrid and stinking, catching at the breath. There was nil visibility, but the radar was keeping track of the enemy, as the enemy would be keeping track of the *Caithness*: as if in proof of this, the accuracy of the gunfire appeared to increase as the Japanese gunlayers came on to the radar bearings at last. A near miss fell astern, not far behind the depth-charges in the racks. The *Caithness* shook like a duck waggling its tail. The stern lifted and dropped again and the hull seemed to vibrate alarmingly. Then another, close to the starboard side for'ard. A spout of water rose through the murk, coming inboard and drenching the bridge personnel.

'Getting close, sir,' Tillotson said.

'Too bloody close, Mid.' Cameron was coming to a final decision: the situation had to be brought to a head now. He moved fast to the aft part of the bridge and shouted down. 'Mr Clinch!'

'Yessir?'

'Stand by your tubes, port and starboard. Report when ready. I'm turning to the attack. The radar shows two of the Japs steaming in line abreast astern of us . . . I'll try to get in between. Get the idea?'

'Yessir,' Clinch shouted back, rubbing his hands together. He'd got the idea all right: fire port and starboard when the bridge came on to the bearing, or thought it did, and try to take two of the yellow perils with them. They could have a chance. Mr Clinch passed his order to his torpedo party, missing Inman, the LTO. He would need to be in two places at once, with Inman gone. However, he would cope. He saw the tubes trained to port and starboard, the triple mountings

177

swinging round to the beam, pointing menacingly into the murk. In the wheelhouse Chief PO Chapman put the helm hard over in response to orders from the bridge and then steadied on a reciprocal of the earlier course to head right into the guns of the Japs.

'Proper Charge o' the Light Brigade is this,' he remarked to the telegraphsman. 'Guns to the right of us, guns to the left of us – or soon will be. Best keep your head down, son.'

'It's bleeding daft, chief. . . .'

'Not all that daft. Anything can happen on a night like this and I reckon the skipper has a sporting chance of getting away with it.'

Below in the engine-room Mr Henty didn't think they had a hope. Cameron had told him on the phone what he was going to do. Mr Henty's eyes held a haunted look, and he kept glancing up through the shining network of steel ladders that zig-zagged their way to the air-lock that formed the one and only way out of the engine-room and the boiler-room too. Just one exit, and too many men making for it when the crunch came. It was always the same in the engine spaces and the fear was always lurking at the back of the mind. If it came further in as it were, if it was thought about too much, you'd go round the bend for sure. But at times, and this was one, you had to make a bigger than ever effort to keep it at bay. Of course, there could be other exits – in the ship's side, brought about by projectiles entering, but that would be sod-all help since the weight of water crashing through would smash you in seconds if you hadn't been knocked off by the explosion. Drown, burn or be steam-flayed, you took your choice – or rather, you had it forced on you.

The ship was shaking, vibrating . . . what if the fuel *did* pack up? But they should have enough for a while anyway. Mr Henty didn't think they were going to survive so as to make it back to Trinco in any case, so there wasn't much point in worrying too much about his bunkers. Just as long as they could take a poke at the bloody Japs . . . he admitted to

178

himself that he was dead scared now, but he was RN through and through and he wanted the *Caithness* to give a good account of herself in her last moments. After that, well, he would see for himself whether or not Lieutenant Pegram had had it right. There was even something quite intriguing about the prospect if you forced yourself to think of it that way so you didn't wet your pants at the last. 'Chin up,' Mr Henty said aloud to himself.

v

Now the bearings were widening out on either bow as the *Caithness* closed the gap, flying on clear of the smoke, or what was left of it. So far the Japanese had not altered their formation. The two destroyers as reported were still in line abreast, with the third coming on in rear and in line with the centre point between the two ahead, slap between their courses, a kind of long stop that was going to be difficult to deal with if they managed to get through the fire from the leading ships; as they came up that would intensify and by the time they had gone past there might be little left.

Watching ahead through his binoculars, Cameron saw the gun-flashes that showed the stepping-up of the bombardment. Shells screamed past the sides and overhead.

Cameron picked up the Tannoy. 'We're nearly there,' he said. 'Stand by torpedo-tubes. Number One?'

A voice responded from amidships, a shout only just audible in the crash and roar of the guns from both sides. 'Sir?'

'Continue firing throughout. Point of aim, the bridges.'

An indistinct shout came back. Cameron saw Petty Officer Jago moving as fast as he could, clambering over the soldiers without ceremony as they lay in what shelter they could find, making for Number Two gun just for'ard of the bridge. Reaching it, Jago took over himself from the gunlayer, opening in quarters firing the moment his sight came on.

Cameron saw the result seconds later: a hit on the bridge of the destroyer in rear of the other two. There was a dull glow following the explosion and then flames shot high. In the light of the fast-spreading fire, Cameron saw the destroyer's head paying off to starboard as though she was out of control. He leaned out over the fore screen and shouted down.

'Well done, GI! I think you took the wheelhouse up with it.'

Briefly, Jago glanced up, a grin on his face, blackened all over the anti-flash gear. Then he was firing again, rapid fire that sent the shells flinging across towards the stricken vessel. More falls of shot where they hurt: more fires were breaking out now, and the destroyer was drifting away towards the north. She wasn't going to last long. Once again Cameron used the Tannoy.

'One down, two to go.'

It was trite enough but the words had their effect. Cheering came from the decks, audible between the bursts of gunfire. Many of the troops were on their feet now and yelling imprecations towards the Japanese as the *Caithness* closed the distance between the remaining destroyers and at the tubes Mr Clinch found himself in a muck-sweat of anticipation and sheer excitement. He watched the narrowing gap closely, waiting for the order to come from the bridge. By this time the gunfire was intense, a curtain of explosives flinging across, and there couldn't be many more miracles. A moment after Mr Clinch had this thought something took the bow on the starboard side, and the destroyer's way checked as the night seemed to turn to a fiery red. The explosion rocked the whole ship; her head paid off until the Coxswain, fighting the wheel, brought her back on course. There would be chaos below along the messdecks but the *Caithness* was moving on, now at reduced speed on orders from the bridge: the collision bulkhead, apparently holding, would have to be nursed. Cameron passed orders for the First Lieutenant to leave the guns and check round personally with his damage-control party. Main was seen briefly, coming up from the vicinity of

Four gun, when another shell took the searchlight platform on the midship superstructure and carried it clean away from its mounting while slivers of steel burst around the decks and the close-packed troops. On the bridge Cameron held fast to the binnacle, watching the bearings as the *Caithness* moved on. By his estimate the two Japs were around eight cables apart, and in a sense sitting targets despite the speed closure. If he judged the moment right, the fish couldn't miss. It all depended on that: he must give the order in the exact instant that would bring the targets across the course of the torpedoes to port and starboard so that, in effect, they steamed right into the line of fire.

It was a case of seconds now, seconds that seemed like hours. The whole of the vicinity was in smoke and flame. The third Jap destroyer was still on fire and out of the fight totally, drifted well clear. And now the other two, obviously having ticked over as to what Cameron meant to do, were altering course, both together, each outwards, to port and starboard respectively.

Cameron passed the word to the tubes: '*Fire!*'

On the starboard side, Mr Clinch pulled the firing lever. One away . . . two away . . . three away. The acting LTO did the same on the port side. Mr Clinch wiped sweat from his streaming face as he saw his fish take the water and in the light of the fires and the exploding shells saw the six trails leading nicely away from the side, three to port, three to starboard. It was out of his hands now. For good or ill, they'd shot their last bolt and in the next couple of minutes or so they would know their fate for sure.

vi

Petty Officer Jago had been blown clear off his gunlayer's seat by the blast from the shell that had taken the bow. He tried to pick himself up, swearing in a low monotone as shafts of agony went through his left leg. Bloody broken it was: sod the

Japs! But he was alive, which was something, and intact apart from the leg and no doubt some God Almighty bruises. He set his teeth, dragged his body along the deck plating and heaved himself upright by getting a grip on the centre-line capstan. He made an attempt to hop aft towards Two gun so as to resume his position as gunlayer. The fight wasn't over yet. Sweat broke out all over; the pain was intense but he wasn't going to be beaten. Two of the gun's crew were moving out now, coming to his assistance. They had their arms around his body when the big explosions came to port and starboard, almost simultaneously.

Jago looked around, his leg temporarily forgotten. God alone knew just how many of the fish had hit, but both destroyers were well and truly on fire and in the flames Jago could see that the one to port was well down by the stern, her bow lifting high, while the other was laid over hard to starboard, her decks sharply canted and a swarm of men sliding down into the water. The gunfire had ceased, and the *Caithness* was already slowing. Cheering came from all along the upper deck, the troops going mad, shouting derision, relieving their feelings about a long and cruel imprisonment. On the bridge Cameron decided to let them have their head. They'd deserved this moment and it was not the time or the place to utter words of chivalry . . . he turned to find the chief bosun's mate behind him with questions.

'Survivors, sir. Pick the buggers up – or not? If we do, God knows where we'll put 'em!'

'We'll find room now,' Cameron said. He didn't elaborate but Bustacle had got the drift: the dead would make room for the living. Bustacle had already seen that there were plenty of casualties: the troops had been the worst sufferers, not unexpectedly. A rough count had already shown some forty of them dead, and more probably blown overboard, and there had been casualties to the ship's company when the searchlight platform had been blown out of its mountings. There were more aft by Three and Four guns. Yes, there

182

would be room. Bustacle didn't believe too many of the Japs would have survived the battering of the guns and torpedoes and the resulting fires; and he believed that the number was going to be even less when the listing destroyer suddenly glowed red throughout her plates, and then blew up in a devastating explosion that sent debris flinging high in the night sky and over the decks of the *Caithness*.

'I'll put the nets over for what's left from that lot, sir,' Bustacle said. He made his way aft. If any of the yellow buggers got stroppy, he'd personally shove them back in. It was as he was going aft that he spotted a huddle in a shell-torn gap in the midship superstructure, port side. Damage from when that shell got the searchlight platform above . . . shells and their blast did funny things. The huddle wan't all that obvious and probably hadn't been noticed until now. Bustacle took a closer look, reached out, felt no heartbeat but plenty of blood and burned flesh, all pulpy like an overripe plum that sogged when you put a finger to it. There wasn't a lot left to recognize except for a shoulder-strap with two gold stripes – straight stripes, RN stripes. All that was left of Jimmy the One. An uncharitable thought came to Bustacle and wouldn't go away: Jimmy could have crawled in there for shelter and then got done by another projy landing too close . . . but as to that, they would never know.

vii

'Late but welcome,' Cameron said, looking across the water towards the great, grey bulk of a fleet carrier as it came from the west, already heralded by a squadron of Fulmars flown off in advance of its course. No Japanese reinforcements had been sent out, it seemed, and the *Caithness* had come under no further attack; but now she was limping home, going slow so as to conserve as much of her oil fuel as possible for the haul to Trincomalee and to ease the strain on the fore collision bulkhead. It was going to be a nice feeling, to have the cover of the carrier and her aircraft. Signals were exchanged by light: the carrier's Captain reported that fingers had been pulled out ashore and the destroyer's likely predicament as to fuel had been anticipated. A fleet oiler was being despatched with a corvette escort, and *Caithness* would have her tanks filled for base.

The immediate future thus more or less assured, Cameron, by this time a zombie only just capable of movement, turned in for a spell, leaving the ship in the hands of Midshipman Tillotson. The officer casualties had been devastatingly heavy, with only Tillotson and Mr Clinch left, plus the Doctor and Mr Henty. In the wardroom pantry Able Seaman Urridge was taking his ease when the SBA came in and said the GI wanted words with him in the sick bay. Jago's leg was in plaster and hitched up by a kind of pulley-hauley to some contraption in the deckhead, but Jago himself was back to normal.

'You wanted to see me, GI.'

'Right. Drunk just before action.'

'I never!'

'That's a barefaced lie and you know it, Able Seaman Urridge. See you myself. There's worse. Threats uttered against the First Lieutenant – no, don't you deny it, you rotten lousy matlow, you.' Jago hoisted himself on to one elbow and stared at Urridge. 'Very nasty threats amounting to blackmail.'

Urridge licked at his lips, his face pale. 'You going to make something of it, GI? First Lootenant's dead, which – '

'Yes. And you're going to keep your dirty mouth shut tight, Able Seaman Urridge, or I'll get you. Which means, as you've no doubt realized, that there'll be no charges. I'm not seeing any officer or man slandered when he's dead, killed in action. All right? Charge you, and you'll talk – I'm not having that. So you keep your trap shut, now and for evermore. I'll be on your back till Kingdom come. Same applies to your mate Roebuck. Best tell him, hadn't you?' Jago's voice was hard: Jimmy, he hadn't been a lot of use one way and another, but he had given his life whichever way you looked at it. 'Lucky for some, isn't it,' he said between set teeth. 'You bastard!'